Praise for *Dinosaur Boy*

A Junior Library Guild selection

"A series debut with more twists than a strand of DNA…good fun."
—*Kirkus Reviews*

"A fun and funny read with layers of deeper issues."
—*School Library Journal*

"A fun mix of school drama, science fiction, and humor, the story explores the daily hassles of living as part dinosaur, along with the real pain of bullying. First in a planned series, it should find a wide audience."
—*Booklist*

"And you thought your day at school was rough. *Dinosaur Boy* is a hilarious adventure and as sharp as a stegosaurus's tail, with twists and turns on every page… Fantastic."
—Nathan Bransford, author of *Jacob Wonderbar and the Cosmic Space Kapow*

"Filled with depth and emotion I never saw coming. With issues like bullying, not fitting in, and heroism…It's *Wonder* with dinosaurs and is sure to touch your heart."
—P. J. Hoover, author of *Tut: The Story of My Immortal Life*

"A wild and wacky adventure …sure to appeal to wonderfully weird kids of every shape and size."

—Kelly Milner Halls, award-winning author
of *In Search of Sasquatch* and *Dinosaur Mummies*

"Dinosaur-human hybrids and mysterious visitors from ▮▮▮▮! What more needs to be said? A delightfully zany and terrifically fun story of friendship and how to survive fifth grade with a thagomizer of your very own."

—Greg Leitich Smith, award-winning author of
Chronal Engine and *Little Green Men at the Mercury Inn*

"Funny, fast-paced, and filled with surprising twists, *Dinosaur Boy* is a charming story. The ending will have boys and girls roaring for more of Sawyer's adventures, and possibly wishing for their very own dinosaur genes!"

—Nikki Loftin, author of *The Sinister Sweetness*
of Splendid Academy and *Nightingale's Nest*

DINOSAUR BOY

Cory
Putman
Oakes

sourcebooks
jabberwocky

For Mark, Sophia, and Alexander:
Who I will always love,
exactly as they are.
Spikes and all
(if applicable).

Published by Sourcebooks Jabberwocky, an imprint of Sourcebooks, Inc.
P.O. Box 4410, Naperville, Illinois 60567-4410
(630) 961-3900
Fax: (630) 961-2168
www.sourcebooks.com

The Library of Congress has cataloged the hardcover edition as follows:

Oakes, Cory Putman.
 Dinosaur boy / Cory Putman Oakes.
   pages cm
 Summary: Sprouting a tail and spikes over the summer before fifth grade, Sawyer, a boy with the dinosaur gene, is bullied in school, but when his tormentors begin to disappear, it is up to Sawyer, his best friend Elliot, and a mysterious new girl to rescue them from a galactically horrible fate.
 [1. Stegosaurus--Fiction. 2. Dinosaurs--Fiction. 3. Bullying--Fiction. 4. Extraterrestrial beings--Fiction. 5. Rescues--Fiction. 6. Schools--Fiction.] I. Title.
 PZ7.1.O15Di 2015
 [Fic]--dc23

                    2014030138

Source of Production: Versa Press, East Peoria, Illinois, USA
Date of Production: October 2016
Run Number: 5007827

Printed and bound in the United States of America.
VP 10 9 8 7 6

The Dinosaur Gene

It all started with a bump. A little one. Right on the back of my neck.

It didn't hurt or anything. It was just a bump.

"Did something bite you?" my dad asked when I showed him.

"No," I said.

"Hmmm." My dad scratched his head. "Well, I'm sure it'll go away soon."

But it didn't. And about a week later, a second bump appeared, just a little bit lower on my neck than the first one and slightly to the side. Then another one came.

And another one.

And another one. Until I had two lines of bumps running straight down my back.

That was when my tail started growing.

I wasn't quite as surprised by this as you might think. After all, my grandfather had been part stegosaurus. And everybody knows that dinosaur skips a generation, so I had always been warned that something like this might happen to me.

But I didn't know that it was going to happen so fast.

My family spends every summer in our cabin next to Lake Siesta, outside of Portland. This summer, on the car ride there, I noticed my first bump. By the end of our third week at the lake, I had seventeen bumps and a tail stump that made it very difficult to sit down.

My mother was *thrilled*. She spent a lot of that summer on the phone with her sister in Wisconsin, bragging that *her* kid had "the dinosaur gene." None of my cousins had ever been able to boast as much as a single spike. Or even a patch of skin that seemed particularly leathery. When Mom wasn't talking to Aunt Carol, she was busy cutting holes in the back of all of my jeans so that my tail could fit through.

"It's like I always say," she said happily, from behind the sewing machine. "At least it isn't boring. Never a dull moment. Right, Sawyer?"

Easy for her to say.

My dad didn't say much about the whole dinosaur thing. But then, he wasn't a big talker in general. He took me fishing every morning, but the only thing he ever said to me on those trips was to be sure not to tangle the line and to be quiet so that we wouldn't scare the fish away.

I didn't mind not talking about it. Mostly because I wasn't quite as thrilled about the whole thing as my mom was. For one thing, it kind of started to hurt. The bumps on my neck and back grew into triangle-shaped plates that were each about the size of my hand.

They were heavy and sore and very uncomfortable. Especially when I accidentally rolled over on them in the middle of the night. And I don't know if you've ever grown a tail or not, but if you haven't, just let me tell you: it's not fun.

One time, when I was in the second grade, I fell off a fence in my backyard and landed right on my tailbone. My butt hurt for the next two days. That's kind of what the tail felt like, except that it took a lot longer than two days to grow. Basically, I felt like I had just fallen off a fence every day for two months.

Sitting made it much worse, so I spent most of that summer standing up. Even at mealtimes. And boy, did I eat a lot. I was hungry from the moment I got up in the morning until the moment I went to bed at night. It didn't matter how much I ate. I was hungry even *while* I was eating.

At the beginning of the summer, Mom had stocked the cabin with lots of frozen pizza and fried chicken, my two favorites. But I didn't want to eat either of those things anymore. All I wanted were vegetables. Plates and plates of vegetables. Plus salads so big I had to put them in mixing bowls. And so much fruit that we became regulars at several farmers markets around the Portland area.

Pretty soon, not even my biggest clothes could hide what was happening to me. Mom had to cut two long strips down the back of each of my shirts. She also had to enlarge the holes she had already made in the backs of my jeans because my tail had grown thicker.

My tail had also grown so long that I had to be really careful when I turned around suddenly. Especially once four-foot-long, razor-sharp spikes grew out of it. I shredded two rugs and the side of a couch, plus I did untold damage to the wood floor in the entryway before my dad had the idea of skewering a tennis ball onto the end of each spike. After that, I made little bouncy sounds whenever I walked on hard surfaces, but I no longer left a trail of destruction behind me. And everybody got a lot less nervous about accidentally startling me.

The plates eventually stopped being sore all the time. And they turned from an angry red color to a mild, pleasant green. My tail was a slightly darker shade of green. The skin from my neck, down my back, all the way to the tip of my tail became hard, like really thick leather. But that was okay by me, because it made my plates and my tail feel a lot less heavy.

All things considered, I was adjusting pretty well to my new circumstances. Our cocker spaniel, Fantasia (Fanny for short), even stopped barking at me. It wasn't until mid-August, when we were packing the car to go back home, that a very dark thought occurred to me.

I was going to have to go back to school.

Plates, tail, spikes, and all.

Last summer, the one before fourth grade, my best friend Elliot grew five whole inches. And once school started, the other kids in our class teased him like crazy. They gave him nicknames like "Stretch" and "Gigantor" and "the Jolly Green Giant." It didn't really let up until we started our basketball unit in gym, and suddenly everybody wanted Elliot on their team.

Something told me that my plates, my tail, and my spikes were going to be a bigger deal than Elliot's five inches. And I was pretty sure that nobody was going to want me on their basketball team.

Fitting In

My mom didn't understand why I would be nervous on my first morning back to school as a part-dinosaur.

"Sweetie," she said, bending down to fold the collar of my polo shirt underneath my top-most plate. I shivered; the holes in the back of my shirt made it a bit drafty. "You have a gift that is extraordinarily rare. You should be proud! Tell me you're proud to be who you are."

"Sure," I said.

My dad gave me slightly different advice.

"Don't let the other kids give you a hard time," he told me. "Hold your head up high; make every kid in your class wish that *they* had plates and a tail."

Since my dad seemed to be somewhat more aware of the reality of my situation than my mom, I decided to repeat his words to myself as I grabbed my lunch and headed for the front door. My mom ran after me with my jacket, which she had just finished altering to fit over my plates. When I turned so she could help me into it, she drew in a sharp breath.

"Sawyer!" she admonished. "Have you lost a tennis ball?"

I looked over my shoulder. One of my spikes had indeed managed to shake itself loose of its protective covering and was now alarmingly exposed, in all of its razor-sharp glory. Behind me, there was a long gash in the carpet that marked the path I had taken from the kitchen to the hallway.

I tried to think how the tennis ball could have come off. I couldn't recall getting it stuck on anything.

But before I could wrack my brain too hard, Fanny came tearing out of the kitchen. She streaked by my mom and me and ran upstairs, a yellow tennis ball clenched securely in her jaws and an unmistakable gleam of triumph in her large brown eyes.

I sighed. From the beginning, the only flaw in the tennis ball plan had been Fanny's rabid love for them. And ever since we had returned home from the lake, she had been growing increasingly bold in her attempts to steal them off my spikes.

I heard my mom sigh too.

"Sorry," I said guiltily.

Mom looked down at the torn-up carpet and bit her lip.

"No worries, dear. Let's just get it back on and then get you to school. OK?"

That turned out to be easier said than done. We were out of extra tennis balls, and Fanny was not at all inclined to give hers up. When we were unable to coax her out from underneath my parents' bed, where she had hidden to chew her prize in peace, we had no choice but to stop at a sporting goods store on the way to school to buy a replacement. That made me officially late. By the time I had skewered the new tennis ball onto the exposed spike and walked into my class-room, the bell had rung and everybody else was already in their seats. The door to the classroom was in the back, and all the desks were facing the front. So when the door thumped shut behind me, every single kid in my class turned around in his or her seat.

To stare at me.

I felt my heart start to beat faster. I had kind of expected this, given my new dinosaur-ness, but that didn't make it any easier to handle. I have never been one of those kids who likes attention. If I could have disintegrated into a puddle on the floor and disappeared, I would have.

But I couldn't. Instead, I just had to stand there. With my dinosaur-ness on full display. So that everybody could get a good, long look.

I tried not to stare back at anyone, but suddenly it seemed like there was nowhere safe for me to rest my eyes.

I was relieved to finally find Elliot in the crowd. He was sitting in the back row with his long legs stretched out into the aisle. And he was smiling at me. Instead of staring with his mouth open like everybody else.

To be fair, Elliot had been receiving email updates (complete with pictures) on my "condition" all summer. And the rest of the class hadn't.

When our eyes met, Elliot gave me a head nod and a wave. As though there was nothing unusual going on that day at all.

I knew I'd be able to count on Elliot.

"Hello," came a voice from the front of the room. "You must be Sawyer. I am Ms. Filch."

I looked up, and at first I had a hard time finding our teacher. That was because she was sitting on the floor at the front of the room beside a large TV, angrily punching buttons on an old-looking DVD player.

She held up one long, bony finger and pointed to an empty seat in the front row.

"Please take your seat. I'll be with you as soon as I get this figured out."

I looked uncertainly at where she had pointed. It was the only unoccupied seat in the room. There were five rows of desks between me and it, with only a narrow aisle between them.

There was no way my dinosaur butt was going to fit through there.

I wasn't sure what to do, so I just stood where I was.

Ms. Filch continued to fight with the DVD player. The TV screen remained blank, and she began to mutter under her breath.

Clearly, she did not appreciate my dilemma.

My classmates didn't seem to get it either. Most of them were throwing me confused stares and exchanging glances that clearly said, *What's his problem?* Even Elliot looked at me questioningly.

I turned slightly so that he could see the width of my tail.

Elliot nodded in understanding. He pulled his legs out of the aisle and scooted his desk a few inches to the left. Then he threw a meaningful look at Gary Simmons, the second tallest kid in our class, who sat on the other side of the aisle. Gary hurried to copy Elliot and moved his desk a few inches out of the way. So did the kids sitting in the other four rows.

Relieved, I walked carefully up the slightly wider aisle toward my desk. Kids leaned out of the way to avoid my plates. Emma Hecht, who sat directly behind the empty desk I was headed for, gave a tiny shriek as one of my tennis balls bounced off her sparkly pink Converse. Other than that, there was total silence.

Until the whispers started.

"Unreal," I heard someone murmur behind me.

"Gross," I heard someone else say.

"Wow," a third somebody breathed. "Just...wow."

"Do all dinosaurs have tennis balls?"

That last one had to be Ernie Hobbs. He'd been in my class since kindergarten, and he'd never been very smart.

By then, I had made it to the front row. I felt a tiny surge of pride at my achievement...which quickly faded when I got a good look at my desk.

It was the kind with a small writing surface that was bolted to the front of a chair. I had sat in just this sort of desk since first grade, but I had never noticed until this morning just how *small* they were.

All the eyes in the room, except for Ms. Filch's, remained on me. I started to sweat as I formed a plan. All I had to do was get myself into my seat. Then class would start and everybody would forget about me for a little while.

Be smooth, I told myself. *Be cool.*

I was going to have to go in spikes first, that much was obvious. So I turned slightly to the side and reached down (smoothly, coolly) to grab the end of my tail.

But I missed. My tail whipped to the opposite side, like it was purposely trying to do the least helpful thing that it could. I turned the other way, to try and grab it before it could hit anything, but it was too late. One of my tennis-balled spikes caught the straps of Emma's pink Hello Kitty backpack and flung it halfway across the room, spraying papers and hair clips in all directions.

"Oh no!" I whipped around to apologize to her, which made my tail swing high in the opposite direction. It knocked all the books off the desk to my right.

"Oh! I'm so sorry!" I exclaimed, fighting the urge to turn quickly and face the desk's occupant, Parker Douglas. Remaining absolutely still was the only thing I could think of that would prevent the further destruction of my immediate area.

"Dude, be careful with that thing!" Parker grumbled. I didn't have to look at him to know that he was probably scowling. Parker, the skinniest kid in our entire grade, always had a long face. Partly because his face was literally very long and oval-shaped. And partly because he frowned a lot.

"Chill, Parker." Emma scolded him from behind me. "It's not like he hurt anyone."

She gave me a tiny smile as she jumped out of her seat, and I watched enviously as she zigzagged easily through the desks, picking up her stuff as she went.

"I'm really sorry," I muttered to them both.

Just get in your seat! I ordered myself. *This will all be over once you get your butt in your chair!*

Gritting my teeth, I turned to the side once more, willing my tail to cooperate. This time, I was able to grab it and thread the spikes through the square-shaped opening in the back of the chair. The tennis balls bounced slightly as my spikes hit the floor, making my tail do a little dance.

There were muffled giggles behind me.

My cheeks felt like they were on fire. They must have been bright red by now, which probably made me look even more ridiculous. The tips of my plates also felt hot, like they were embarrassed too.

I was still only halfway in my chair, so I had no choice but to turn my back on the gigglers and sit down. I sucked in a breath and wedged myself painfully into the narrow space between the desk and the chair. In order for all of my plates to fit, I had to sit with the front of my chest pressed uncomfortably against the edge of the desk. I was crammed in so tightly I couldn't even take a deep breath. And several of my plates were bent at strange angles.

Was I going to have to sit like this for the entire day?

Before I could worry about it too much, there was a loud scraping sound to my right. Parker, having piled his books back onto his desk, was now scooting his chair a few inches away from mine. His too-close-together eyes dared me to say something about it.

I looked away, over toward Mary Bishop, who had the desk on the other side of me for the second year in a row. Mary was staring straight ahead. Her right eye twitched a little, which I think meant she knew that I was looking at her. But she didn't turn to look at me.

Instead, she curled the end of her long, black ponytail lazily around one finger. And, keeping her eyes on the front of the room, she dug her feet into the ground and slid her desk a few inches to the left.

I thought that was kind of unfair. After all, I had never tried to move away from Mary. Not even last year, after she ate three fish tacos and a blueberry banana smoothie for lunch and then threw up all over both of our desks. You'd think that if I could forgive her for a lapful of purple guck with little bits of chewed-up fish floating in it, she could forgive me for being part dinosaur. But I guess not…

"Ahhh, there we go," Ms. Filch said, as she finally stood up and turned to face us, remote in hand. "Principal Mathis has asked that we start off the year with a little movie. Every class in the school will be watching this today, but we're the lucky ones who get to see it first. Ernie, can you get the lights please?"

An excited murmur ran through the room. Movies, even boring ones, were *always* better than real class. I couldn't turn around enough to see, but Ernie must have managed to get the lights because a pleasant semidarkness fell over the room. I could only see vague outlines of all the kids around me.

For the first time that morning, I felt myself relax. As much as I possibly could, in my extremely uncomfortable chair. I even had the cheery thought that maybe, just maybe, the worst part of my day was over.

But then, Ms. Filch started the movie.

The Dinosaur in Your Classroom

A giant, green cartoon dinosaur appeared on the screen. Below its huge, obnoxious grin were the words:

The Dinosaur in Your Classroom

An Educational Video from Amalgam Labs

There were bursts of giggles all around me.

I cringed.

The dinosaur faded and was replaced by a tall, skinny woman in a lab coat. She smiled prettily at the camera.

"Hello, boys and girls. My name is Dr. Dana, of Amalgam Labs."

On the bottom of the screen was the disclaimer: *Some scientists portrayed by professional actors.*

"Dr. Dana" continued, in a soothing and falsely cheerful voice. The kind of voice that adults use when they are about to tell kids something they know we won't like.

"I'm here today to talk to you about something you may have

already noticed. That's right! It's time to have an honest and important discussion about the dinosaur in your classroom!"

There was another round of giggles, as several shiny, metallic buildings appeared on the screen.

"This is Amalgam Labs," Dr. Dana chirped. "Once an industry leader in the emerging field of DNA hybridization. DNA hybridization? What in the world is *that*, you ask?"

Dr. Dana came back on the screen, smiling patiently.

"It's simple, really. DNA is a molecule that exists inside of every living creature. Here's what a DNA molecule looks like."

A picture appeared of something that looked like a ladder that had been stretched out and twisted.

"DNA is a very special material because it contains the instructions for how every creature is built. These instructions are called 'genes.' 'DNA hybridization' means combining the genes from two different creatures to create an entirely new DNA strand. Just like the DNA of the dinosaur-human hybrid in your classroom."

Amalgam Labs came back onto the screen.

"Due to numerous ongoing lawsuits and the closing of our main facility in the United States after the passing of the International Treaty on Responsible DNA Research, we may never know exactly how the dinosaur-human hybrid serum was created. Or exactly who was responsible for injecting that serum into a virus and for putting that virus into the ice-cream maker in the laboratory's cafeteria. But what we *do* know is that the DNA of the two hundred and thirty-eight scientists who ingested the ice cream was changed forever."

I risked a quick, stiff-necked glance around the room. My

classmates were riveted, even though I knew they had all heard the story of Amalgam Labs before. We all had. Even the kids whose grandfathers hadn't worked there.

"So what happened to the scientists who ate the ice cream?" Dr. Dana continued. "Well, nothing at first!"

The screen image now showed two men, standing side by side. They were both wearing lab coats.

"The man on the left is Dr. Otto Marsh, one of the scientists who ate the ice cream. The man on the right is Dr. Edwin Cope, one of the three lactose-intolerant scientists at Amalgam Labs who did *not* eat the ice cream. This is what they looked like the day after the incident."

Then two new pictures appeared. The scientist on the right looked exactly the same. But the scientist on the left now had a huge, bony frill growing out of his neck. It framed his face, kind of like a huge shirt collar.

A shirt collar with horns.

"Within one month, 98 percent of the scientists who were infected with the virus began to display external dinosaur features. Just like Dr. Marsh. Once fully developed, these features became permanent, fusing with the existing human features and creating a hybrid-like appearance."

Another picture of Dr. Marsh, with his bony frill, filled the screen. Now, he was bouncing a small (and seemingly human) child on his knee.

"With the help of the Amalgam Labs psychological team, most of the affected scientists were able to adapt to their changed appearances and lead relatively normal lives. One hundred and seventy-two of the scientists went on to produce offspring, all of which grew to maturity without manifesting a single dinosaur characteristic. Therefore, it was concluded that the hybrid DNA was not transferable to subsequent generations."

Dr. Dana came back on the screen, smiling a knowing smile.

"But as we all know, that wasn't the end of the story. Imagine our surprise when the *next* generation of offspring, the grandsons and granddaughters of the affected scientists, started to develop dinosaur characteristics!"

Two kids appeared. The one on the left was an ordinary, if slightly nerdy-looking kid in baggy jeans and glasses. The one on the right had a long, spiny tail, much like mine. He also had very short arms, which were pulled close to his body, and tiny hands with curved claws.

"The boy on the left is Dr. Cope's grandson. In every way, an ordinary human, just like you and me. The boy on the right is Dr. Marsh's grandson. As you can see, he exhibits several remarkably distinct dinosaur characteristics."

And just in case we couldn't see, two enormous flashing arrows appeared, pointing to the boy's tail and arms.

"Today, there are several dozen dinosaur-human hybrids in schools across the country."

A slideshow of various dinosaur-human kids began. Most, like me, were recognizably human with only a few dinosaur traits, like claws or tails. One girl had plates that looked identical to mine, and one very unfortunate boy had a giant triceratops horn where his nose should have been.

"As part of the class action judgment enacted against us, Amalgam Labs has agreed to assist these schools in coming up with effective strategies for the assimilation of dinosaur-hybrid students. We at Amalgam Labs believe that there is no reason that human and semi-human students cannot coexist in a nurturing, safe, and fun learning environment. The following are some tips that fully human students should keep in mind."

A picture of a normal-looking boy appeared. He had his arm around a classmate, who had a beak for a nose and several horns.

"First and foremost, it's important to realize that your hybrid classmate is not contagious. Dinosaur-human hybrids are born, not infected. There is no way that you can catch the dinosaur gene by engaging in normal, day-to-day interactions with your hybrid class-mate. There is no need for schools to provide separate bathroom facil-ities for hybrids."

Up popped a school picture of a boy who looked perfectly normal and well groomed, except for his giant teeth and the bumps all over his forehead.

"Don't judge a book by its cover! Just because your classmate looks a little bit different than he did in last year's school picture, don't forget that *dinosaur-human hybrids are people too*. And they should be treated with the same respect as your fully human classmates."

Next came a picture of a girl with a huge finlike growth down her back. She was performing a complicated math equation in front of a group of human children.

"In most cases, hybrids retain the brain size and IQ measurements they had before their dinosaur characteristics emerged. So don't worry! Your hybrid classmate is mentally the same person he or she always was!"

Next came a picture of the kid with the big teeth and forehead bumps, stomping his feet angrily. A cartoon bubble appeared over his head with the word "ROAR!" in it.

"Remember that any odd behavior exhibited by your hybrid class-mate is *not their fault*. Try not to embarrass your hybrid classmate by drawing unnecessary attention to any of their actions that may not be as common among your fully human classmates."

Now came a picture of a human girl with her arm around the shoulder of another girl who had a full tyrannosaurus rex head.

"Our research has shown that hybrids are unlikely to become violent. However, should the dinosaur in your classroom exhibit any aggressive behavior, please remain calm and immediately inform the nearest adult. Employees at schools where a hybrid has been enrolled have been trained to deal with just this kind of situation."

A picture of what looked like a large water gun flashed on the screen.

"Nearly harmless, fast-acting tranquilizer darts have been issued to one of every three teachers in schools with a hybrid in attendance. And don't you worry! Should the tranquilizer become necessary, in the sole judgment of a licensed, adult carrier, your hybrid classmate will awaken in four to six hours, feeling refreshed and calm."

I sneaked a sideways glance at Ms. Filch. Was she "one of every three" who had a tranquilizer gun in her classroom? And if so, where did she keep it? She didn't look terribly thrilled at the idea that it might one day be her responsibility to shoot me with a tranquilizer dart. But I might have just been imagining things.

"In conclusion," Dr. Dana continued, as a class photo depicting a group of grinning students, including one whose enormous tail was curled over the toes of the other kids in the front row, came onto the screen, "as long as appropriate safety guidelines are rigorously enforced, there is no reason your hybrid classmate cannot be an active member of your school community. On behalf of all of us at Amalgam Labs, I wish you a safe and productive school year!"

The movie ended with a picture of what must have been the Amalgam Labs logo: two of the twisted ladders, one red and one green, in the process of being fused together.

I tried to slump down in my chair, but my plates wouldn't let me sink down more than an inch or two.

I tried to recall the advice my dad had given me, about holding my head up high. But somehow, his words didn't sound quite as compelling as they had that morning in our kitchen. After that movie, there was no way that a single one of my classmates was ever going to wish they had plates and a tail.

I was beginning to wish that I didn't either.

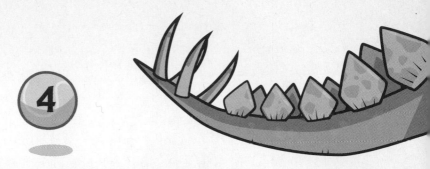

Butt Brain

The next day, our first subject was computer lab. I walked there with Elliot.

Since the day Elliot discovered basketball, he hadn't left his house without looking like a temple to the sport that had finally made school bearable for him. And it looked like things were going to be no different this year. Today, he was wearing the Portland Trail Blazers jersey I had gotten him for his birthday and black high-top basketball shoes. He was even carrying a basketball. Probably for extra insurance, just in case summer break had caused some of the kids to forget that he was, in fact, a basketball player, as opposed to just "that tall freak."

I had been the only person who had stuck by Elliot while everyone else was calling him "Jolly Green Giant" and asking him how the weather was up there. We had been friends since kindergarten, and I had always figured that he would have done the same for me.

I guess I was about to find out if that was true.

"Do you think you'll ever get used to your plates and stuff?" he asked me, and reached over to touch my topmost one. But he pulled his hand back at the last second. He looked a tad embarrassed, and I could practically hear Dr. Dana's cheerful assurances that I was "not contagious" playing through his head.

"I don't know," I said vaguely, and turned back toward the computer lab, like I hadn't noticed anything. Elliot fell in beside me, dribbling his basketball from hand to hand as we walked. When we were little, people had sometimes asked if Elliot and I were twins. Probably because we had the same dirty blond hair and hazel eyes. Plus, we both had a ton of freckles. But that had been before Elliot's five inches and my dinosaur parts.

I doubted that anyone would mistake us for twins now.

"Do they hurt?" Elliot asked.

"Not anymore," I said, looking at the floor. Looking up at Elliot had been a pain since his growth spurt. Now, with my plates, it was nearly impossible.

"Well, that's good. I guess," he said uncomfortably. "And it's definitely…you know…permanent?"

"Looks like it."

"Hmmmm," he said, opening the computer lab door. "Bummer."

Mr. Broome, our computer teacher, yawned at the sight of us. Mr. Broome suffered from crippling allergies, so he was always either sneezing like crazy or about to fall asleep because of his medication. Not long after we had all filed into the room, he muttered something about us having "free lab time," put his head down on the desk, and drifted off.

I turned to ask Elliot what he wanted to do. But he just gestured sadly to the empty chairs on either side of us.

The rest of the class had decided to give us a three-computer buffer, on both sides.

I just shrugged, as though it didn't matter. Elliot shrugged back, as though he didn't care either.

There were a bunch of kids gathered around a computer in the row ahead of us. Allan Huxley stood right in the middle of the group.

Like Elliot, Allan had been in my class since kindergarten. But unlike Elliot, Allan and I had never been friends. A certain alleged pants-wetting incident back in first grade had made *that* pretty much impossible.

Not that I would have wanted to be Allan's friend anyway. Allan had been the leader of the group that had tormented Elliot last year.

He seemed excited about something just then, which worried me. His head, which was so big that it made the rest of his body look small, whipped around to stare at me.

I looked away, as alarm bells started going off in my brain.

"No, that's not it," he said, turning back to the computer screen. "He doesn't have a neck thingy."

In direct defiance of the many NO FOOD OR DRINKS signs that were posted around the lab, he stuffed a wad of beef jerky into his mouth and started chewing it. Noisily.

At least, I thought it was beef jerky. Allan's dad was a big hunter and made his own deer jerky, so it might have been that. Ugh. Even before my dino gene had made me a vegetarian, the thought of eating dried Bambi strips would have made me want to barf.

"What about that one?" Parker asked, reaching a skinny arm around Allan to point at the screen. There were too many heads in the way for me to see what he was talking about.

"Can't be that one," Allan argued, his mouth still full. "He doesn't have anything on his head. What about—"

"There!" Cecilia Craig interrupted. Cecilia, who preferred to be called Cici, shoved both boys out of the way so she could stick her rather prominent nose right into the thick of things. She gestured triumphantly at the screen. "*That's* totally it."

All of the heads around the computer turned to look at me.

"*Stegosaurus*," Allan said, grinning so hard I thought his face might rip apart. He had really thick eyebrows, which sort of loomed over both of his eyes so that even his smiles tended to look like frowns. "Definitely *Stegosaurus*."

"I could have told you that," I muttered. "I know what I am."

"Nobody asked you, Spiky," Allan said, and turned back to the computer. "Let's see. Stegosaurus. *A big but gentle herbivore from the late Jurassic period. Identifiable by two rows of bony plates and a spiked tail… Could have weighed up to four tons…native to western North America…*"

"Boring," Cici singsonged. She flung her hair back over her shoulder, spraying a few drops of water in my direction. Cici had swim practice every morning before school, so her long, mousy brown hair was always a little bit damp. "Skip to the good stuff."

"*Stegosaurus had an unusually small head*," Allan continued. "*with a brain roughly the size of a walnut—*"

"A walnut!" Parker exclaimed, turning to fix his beady eyes on me. He was scowling, as usual, and he looked just as mean as the

Angry Bird on his bright red shirt. "You hear that, Sawyer? Did it hurt when your brain shrank?"

"Shut up, Parker," Elliot said loyally. "Obviously his brain didn't shrink."

"Stay out of it, Gigantor," Cici hissed. "We'll look up what kind of dinosaur you are next."

"I am *not* a dinosaur," Elliot fumed, then immediately looked guilty. He turned to me. "Sorry, Sawyer. It's not that I'd mind being one. It's just that I'm—"

"You guys, you *guys*," Allan interrupted, waving everybody silent. "Listen to this: *Because of its small head size and the existence of a mysterious cavity in its upper hip region, some scientists have theorized that Stegosaurus had a supplementary brain located in its hindquarters.*"

"A supplementary brain?" Cici sniffed. "In its hindquarters? You mean its—"

"Butt," Allan finished, turning around so that I could see the victorious grin on his oversized face. "I mean its *butt*. This article is saying that Spiky here probably has a brain *in his butt*."

Every kid in the room, except for Elliot and me, started laughing hysterically. I stared down at the keyboard in front of me, burning with embarrassment. I couldn't look up. Especially when, over the deafening laughter, I heard Parker start chanting, "Butt Brain! Butt Brain! Butt Brain!"

It had been a huge mistake to come back to school.

I sneaked a glance over at Mr. Broome, but he was still passed out like a useless lump. At that point, I doubt he could have done anything to bring the room back to order anyway. Elliot's weak protests on my behalf were being drowned out by Allan's booming laughter and Cici's deafening cackle. Out of the corner of my eye, I saw Parker stand up on a chair. His red shirt hung loosely on his skinny frame as he raised his hands like a conductor and led his whole side of the room in the Butt Brain chant.

I closed my eyes. I couldn't see anything, so I actually *felt* the icy chill of the outside air before I saw who was responsible for letting it in.

"*SILENCE!*" a voice rang out.

I opened my eyes.

The voice, part yowling cat and part booming cannon, caused everybody in the room to freeze. Parker stopped gesturing so abruptly that he almost fell off his chair.

An extremely small, skinny woman with extremely large, poofy hair stood in the doorway. She was wearing a very stiff-looking suit and glasses that were so large they took up most of her face. She nodded at Mr. Broome, who was blinking sleepily at her from behind his desk.

"So sorry to wake you," she said gravely.

"What? Oh, uh, not at all, Principal Mathis," Mr. Broome stammered. He cleared his throat loudly and struggled to sit up straight.

Principal Mathis...so *this* was our new principal. Principal Kline, our last principal, had resigned suddenly in the middle of the summer and none of us had seen his replacement.

Until now.

Principal Mathis turned away from Mr. Broome. Her eyes, squinting behind her enormous glasses, scanned the room until they came to rest on Parker.

"What is your name, young man?"

"P–P–Parker Douglas," he answered, and I thought I saw his knees start to shake.

"Mr. Douglas," she said. Her voice was so quiet now, we all had to strain to hear her over the crushing silence. "I see you have come up with a new nickname for one of your classmates."

"It wasn't me," Parker choked out. "We were just looking some stuff up—"

"What was it?"

Parker, still up on the chair, pointed down at the computer.

"Just a website on types of—"

"No," Principal Mathis said quietly. "The name. What was it?"

"B–B–Butt Brain," he stammered. And even in the midst of his terror, for tiny Principal Mathis was truly terrifying at that moment, I saw a small smile tug at the edge of his lips.

I don't know if Principal Mathis saw it too. I'm not sure it would have made any difference.

"I believe you are aware, Mr. Douglas, that we have a zero tolerance policy at this school regarding the belittling and harassment of students?"

"Yes, ma'am," Parker mumbled. The smile was suddenly gone from his face.

"And you would agree, I assume, that name-calling is a form of belittling? And also harassment?"

"Yes, ma'am," Parker mumbled, barely audible now.

"Thank you, Mr. Douglas," Principal Mathis said flatly. "Please come with me."

She turned toward the door.

Parker climbed self-consciously down from the chair. He took a step toward Principal Mathis, then froze again as she suddenly turned back around.

"Bring your things. You shan't be returning."

Now that Parker wasn't hurling insults at me, I felt almost sorry for him as he stooped down to pick up his backpack. He looked very small and pathetic as he exchanged a miserable look with Allan and then followed Principal Mathis out of the door.

5

The Zero Tolerance Policy

At the end of the day, just before the final bell, I received a note that I was wanted in Principal Mathis's office.

When I entered the administration building, I shivered at the excessive air-conditioning. And the first person I saw was Ms. Helen.

I'm not sure what Ms. Helen's actual job was. She never seemed busy. But every time I walked into the administrative office, there she was. Wearing a sleeveless top and sitting perfectly still right beneath the air-conditioner vent. The only things on her desk were a huge fan, which was always aimed directly at her face, and a small model solar system. And Ms. Helen couldn't have known that much about space, because her model was totally out of date; there were nine planets in it.

Nobody had ever seen her get up from her desk. Not even to go to the bathroom.

Ms. Helen nodded gravely at me as I passed her. She didn't seem alarmed that a half-dinosaur had just walked into the office. She must have known I was coming.

Principal Mathis met me at the door of the office that, until this summer, had belonged to Principal Kline. I was still a little bit confused about what had happened to him. The school had sent around a letter telling us that he had won the Oregon Lottery and retired. I had always liked Principal Kline, and I had thought he liked us too, but the letter had also said that the good-bye note he had left behind had been "inappropriate to share with the students."

Even in her extremely tall shoes and with her very poofy hair, Principal Mathis was only about an inch or two taller than me. I didn't have to crane my neck to look up at her, the way I did with most adults.

Which was a good thing. Because now that I had bony plates sticking out of my neck, craning of any kind was really out of the question.

"Hello, Sawyer," Principal Mathis said, shaking my hand and giving me a smile that showed all of her teeth. She kept a grip on my hand and pulled on my arm so that I did a half turn, allowing her to look at me from the side.

"My, my," she admired. "What lovely plates."

"They're very rare, you know," said a familiar voice from inside the office.

Principal Mathis stepped to one side, and my mom smiled at me from one of the two chairs in front of a large desk.

"Less than 0.008 percent of the population has the dinosaur gene," my mom added, giving me a small wave.

"Yes, I know," Principal Mathis said, gesturing for me to enter and take the empty seat next to my mom, as she walked to the other side of the desk and sat down in a large swivel chair. "And only 0.15 percent of that number actually manifests any external dinosaur traits. We at Jack James Elementary School consider ourselves *extremely* lucky to be one of the only schools in the country to have such an extraordinary student among us."

My mother beamed.

I stared hard at the nameplate on Principal Mathis's desk and tried not to die.

"That being said," Principal Mathis said, clearing her throat as she sat forward in her chair. "We can't pretend, Mrs. Bronson, that the change in Sawyer's appearance has gone unnoticed among his peers."

"Of course not," my mother agreed.

"I was hoping to avoid having this meeting, but given the events of earlier today, I thought we should all take a moment to discuss the situation."

"I agree," my mom said gravely. I got the feeling that Principal Mathis had already told her all about what had happened in the computer lab. I wondered if she had also told her about the Butt Brain chant. Suddenly, I felt very small in my chair.

"I think we can expect that Sawyer will continue to attract a great deal of attention from the other students. At least until everybody gets used to it," Principal Mathis continued, pushing her thick glasses farther up her nose. "And not all of the attention will be positive."

My mother waved off the principal's concern with a flick of her hand and gave a resigned laugh.

"Boys will be boys."

Principal Mathis's eyes narrowed.

"Not at this school, Mrs. Bronson."

She turned to me. The lenses in her glasses were so thick they made her eyes look huge. That, along with her weirdly poofy hair, made me think of a not-so-nice nickname for her: Mathis the Mantis.

"Sawyer," she began. She smiled a little bit, which just made her look even more bug-like. "This school has always had a zero tolerance policy regarding bullying. But until now, it has been enforced…well, let's just say sporadically. I intend to change that. As an educator, a safe and cruelty-free learning environment is my top priority. Therefore, any student who harasses, belittles, or threatens another student will be removed from his or her classroom and expelled. No warnings. No second chances. No exceptions. Do you understand?"

"Yes," I mumbled.

"I can't always expect to catch a bully in the act, so I'm going to need your help. If *any student*, *anywhere*, *at any time* gives you trouble, I want you to come straight to me. And I will deal with the problem immediately. Do you understand?"

"Yes," I said again. Even though I knew that I would never, ever rat out one of my classmates. I wasn't stupid. Not being a tattletale was like Rule Number One of elementary school.

Principal Mathis's big bug eyes held mine for a long moment, as though she knew what I was thinking.

Finally, she nodded.

"Wonderful. I'm glad we understand one another."

She turned back to my mother.

"Well, that's all for today. I certainly thank you both for coming in."

"Of course." My mother stood and shook Principal Mathis's hand again. "I'm so happy to know that you'll be looking out for Sawyer."

"It is my privilege," Principal Mathis assured her, walking my mother to the door and showing us both out.

I was less than a foot away from her office when Principal Mathis called after me.

"Sawyer?"

I turned around.

She nodded to the tennis balls on the tips of my spikes and smiled.

"A nice touch, those."

"Thanks," I said.

Her eyes narrowed again.

"Sharp objects that can be used as weapons are prohibited under the school's code of conduct. See that you keep the tennis balls on during school hours."

"Yes, ma'am."

Freak Out

The next morning, the desk next to mine was empty. Parker's things had been removed, and the whole thing had been cleaned out and scrubbed. With bleach, from the smell of things.

I guess Principal Mathis had been serious about that zero tolerance policy thing.

I wasn't sure how I felt about that. Had Parker actually been expelled? Because of me? I wondered if that would make things better or worse.

Wednesday morning was pretty quiet. Allan didn't say a single word to me. Nobody else made fun of me, or sang any songs, or recited any stupid dinosaur facts where I could hear them. The four periods before lunch went by so smoothly that I started to wonder if maybe Principal Mathis was a genius. And maybe Parker's empty seat was serving as a warning to Allan and the others to lay off me, or else.

Then came lunch.

My mom had sent me to school with a large plastic bowl full of salad greens, mandarin oranges, and sliced-up avocado. I was so hungry that I dug right in and gulped down several mouthfuls before I felt the first, sickening *crunch* between my teeth.

Crunch? There wasn't supposed to be anything crunchy in my salad.

Whatever it was, it was stuck between my teeth. I picked it out and examined it. Elliot leaned over to take a look as well.

My stomach lurched when I saw that it had wings, tiny legs, antennae, and an oval-shaped body that I had almost bitten in half.

"Ew! Is that a cricket?" Elliot asked, making a face.

Instead of answering, I gingerly prodded my salad with my fork. I moved aside a couple of pieces of avocado and found more crickets, at least a dozen of them, crawling around the lettuce leaves.

"How did a cricket get into your lunch?" Elliot exclaimed, then paused to double-check that his sandwich was insect-free.

I wondered the same thing, until I remembered that Allan had a pet lizard.

A pet lizard that probably ate crickets.

Elliot gave me the apple from his lunch, but I was still hungry for the rest of the day.

Thursday was even worse. Someone hung a sign that said "AND DINOSAURS" on the door to the girls' bathroom, right underneath the stick figure of the girl. After lunch, another someone tripped me and I fell so hard that one of my plates almost bent in half. And I don't even know when someone attached a pair of pink underwear to one of my tail spikes, because I didn't know they were there until Elliot stopped me in the hallway and ripped them off.

On Friday, the janitor had to bring in a new desk for me, because someone had smeared maple syrup all over my old one, let it dry, and then scratched "BEWARE OF TAR PIT" into it. And that afternoon, a group of kids wearing T. rex masks and carrying water guns followed me home from school. I recognized Allan's enormous head behind one of the masks, and I'm pretty sure Cici was there too. I ran the last three blocks to my house, dragging my sopping wet tail along behind me and wishing I had never even *heard* of fifth grade.

When I finally got home, I ran inside and slammed the door to my house as hard as I could. I half hoped it would make one of those little rectangle panes of glass in it shatter, but it didn't. It just made the wall shake a little.

Apparently, I didn't get to have super-stegosaurus strength. Only the stupid plates and the tail. Just my luck.

"Hello, dear," came my mom's voice from the kitchen. "How was school?"

I stomped upstairs without answering her. Hadn't she heard the slam?

I threw myself into bed, not carring that I was all wet. I curled up on my side with my legs pulled underneath me and my tail curled around my front. It was the only position that was remotely comfortable. I usually slept like this, with pillows wedged on either side of me to hold me in place. I had read somewhere that *Stegosauruses* had probably slept standing up. But that didn't sound comfortable at all. And anyway, those were *real Stegosauruses*. Not hybrid freak dinosaurs, like me.

Fanny, who had been sleeping on the other side of my bed, woke up and started wagging her tail at the sight of me. She shimmied her little brown and white self over so that she could rest her head on my damp leg and continue her nap.

At least *she* didn't care what I looked like. Not now that she had gotten used to me. A big part of me wanted to pet her and tell her all of my problems, the way I had when I was little. But a bigger part of me was not in the mood to cuddle.

Besides, she was probably only snuggling up to me so she could get a chance to steal another one of my tennis balls.

I spotted my laptop on the floor. I reached down to get it, dumping Fanny off me as I did. She whined, quickly righted herself, and then headed back to her original nap spot.

I winced as she scrambled over my tail. The underside was all scraped up and raw from being dragged around all day. The asphalt of the school playground, to say nothing of the sidewalks on my way home, were a lot rougher than the smooth wooden floors at the cabin. Or the carpet in our house. Something a *real* stegosaurus would never have to worry about.

I opened a search engine on the computer just as I smelled my mom come up the stairs. Well, not my mom, precisely, but the fruit salad she was carrying. My tail twitched with excitement at the promise of food.

Fanny opened one eye and watched my tail suspiciously.

My mom opened my door without knocking, holding the bowl of fruit in front of her like a peace offering.

"So, today wasn't any better?" she asked.

I shook my head, not taking my eyes off the computer.

Mom set the bowl of fruit beside me. Still not looking up from the screen, I grabbed a handful of chopped-up apples and stuffed them into my mouth.

"What are you doing?" she asked.

I swallowed.

"Looking up how to make it go away," I said, angling the computer so she could see the search results for "dinosaur gene cure."

Mom sat on the edge of my bed.

"Sweetie," she said gently. "There is no cure."

I grabbed another handful of fruit.

"There *has* to be something," I muttered.

"There isn't," she said. And she sounded so sure that I looked up at her questioningly. I had a sinking feeling.

"You've already checked, haven't you?" I asked.

Mom nodded, looking a teeny bit embarrassed.

"Back at the beginning of the summer when this first started, your father and I looked into it. Just to see what our options were. And it didn't take us long to figure out that there were no options."

"That's not true," I said. "What about surgery? Can't I just get all of this stuff cut off?"

"No," my mom said. "Species-reassignment surgery is unethical. Any doctor who performs it would lose their medical license."

"What about the lab that created the stupid gene in the first place?" I pressed her. "Can't they figure out a way to turn it off?"

"Gene therapy for dinosaur hybrid DNA is still in the testing stages," mom informed me. "They won't reach the human trial stage for at least another five years."

Five years. I'd be in high school by then.

I grabbed another handful of fruit, and Mom put her hand on my shoulder.

"There is no cure, Sawyer, because what you have is not a disease. It's simply who you are."

"No." I shook her hand off, determined not to let her last sentence settle into my brain. "That can't be right. It can't be!"

"Sawyer—" Mom began.

"*I HATE IT!*" I exploded, nearly knocking the computer off my lap. "*I. HATE. IT.*"

I picked up my tail by one of the tennis-balled spikes and threw it off the front of my bed. As though I could make it go away that easily. As though it wasn't attached to me. The sore underside of my tail screamed with pain, but I ignored it. "This can't be who I am! I'm not a f-f-freak!"

My chin wobbled and my eyes filled with tears. All the humiliation of the entire week came down on me at once. The stupid movie. Butt Brain. The crickets. The underwear. And the staring. All week long, there had been the staring. A million questions behind a million staring eyes. But nobody actually talked to me (except Elliot). They'd all rather talk *about* me. Like I wasn't even a person anymore.

My mom set down the fruit bowl, moved my computer out of

the way, and tried to put her arms around me. But I pushed her away and moved to the other side of the bed, over by Fanny.

"I don't want to go back to school," I said, wiping my eyes.

"You have to go to school," Mom said quietly. "It's the law."

"So? Homeschool me!"

"I work, Sawyer," she reminded me. "And so does your father. You'd be alone in the house all day."

"Fine." Actually, that sounded pretty great. "I'll teach myself! Just get me some books or something."

Mom shook her head.

"Our only option is to learn to live with it," she said, standing up. "I'm sorry the first week was hard. But it's bound to get better. You're going to figure this out, Sawyer."

"Sure," I said sarcastically.

I leaned over, grabbed the bowl, and started stuffing fruit into my mouth with both hands.

Mom walked to the door and paused in the door frame to look over her shoulder at me.

"At least it isn't boring," she tried. "Never a—"

"If you say, 'never a dull moment,' I will attack you with my tail spikes," I growled.

My mom pursed her lips. But she knew I didn't mean it.

I didn't. Not really.

"For what it's worth, Sawyer," she said, "you've been part dinosaur since the beginning of the summer, but you never asked me about a cure until today. Do you think this might have more to do with how your classmates feel about it than with how you do?

Maybe it's good you can't make any hasty decisions about surgery or gene therapy that you might regret one day. Maybe it's good that you have some time to get used to it."

I didn't answer her.

Mom sighed.

"How about your grandfather? Maybe it would be helpful for you to talk with someone else who has gone through this? He hasn't responded to any of my messages—you know how he is—but you could try emailing him. He still works for that lab, so maybe he has more information than I do."

I didn't say anything. I just chewed, swallowed, chewed, swallowed, chewed, and swallowed until my mom left and there was no more fruit.

Get used to it?

Was she kidding?

She could get used to it. *I* was going to find a cure.

I retrieved my computer and opened up my email.

From: SBronson@jackjames.com
To: DrSteg@BCemail.com

Dear Grandpa,

This is Sawyer, your grandson. I don't know if Mom told you, but I'm part dinosaur now. And I need to know how not to be.

Please help me. I don't mean any offense. I know you're part stegosaurus too. But you didn't become part dinosaur until you were an adult. It's much harder to do it when you're a kid. School is hard enough.

I really need to find a cure. And you're the only person I can think to ask. Please say you can help me!

Love,
Sawyer

PS The underside of my tail is getting scraped up from being dragged around on the ground all day. Does that happen to you too? What do you do about it?

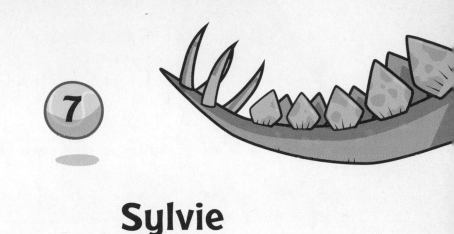

7

Sylvie

On Monday, I didn't want to go to school any more than I had the previous Friday. But my mom marched me through my morning routine with such efficiency that I ended up being the first person to arrive in my classroom.

The only upside to this was that I was able to squeeze into my desk before anybody else got there to witness my horrid awkwardness.

A few minutes before the bell, I heard kids start to arrive and fill up the desks behind me. I sat facing the front of the room, determined not to turn around. Or move. Kind of like in *Jurassic Park*, where the T. rex could only see you if you moved.

Only here, the roles were kind of reversed.

I was concentrating so hard on being invisible that it took me a while to notice that the desk next to mine, which had sat unoccupied for the past week, was no longer empty.

Someone was sitting in Parker's old seat.

I tried to catch a glimpse of the newcomer without turning my head, but all I could see out of the corner of my eye was an oversized sweatshirt the color of a traffic cone. The hood was pulled up, and the owner's face was buried too deep inside for me to be able to catch more than a glimpse. The only thing sticking out was the tip of a nose.

It was red. Like mine got when I forgot to put on sunscreen at the lake.

The newcomer was also wearing white shoes. Really bright white sneakers, without a single scuff. They must have been new.

"Class." Ms. Filch clapped her hands to get our attention. "We have a new student with us. I'd like you all to meet—er, why don't you take off your hood, dear?"

"No," came a determined voice from underneath the sweatshirt.

Ms. Filch looked momentarily startled, but then her face hardened.

"I'm sorry, but I don't allow hats in the classroom."

"I'm not wearing a hat," the figure inside the sweatshirt pointed out. I thought it sounded like a girl's voice, but it was hard to be sure. "I'm wearing a hood. And I like it."

"It's a very lovely, er, color," Ms. Filch said hesitantly, blinking at the neon. "But a hood is the same thing as a hat. And I must insist that you take it off."

The girl—I was slightly more sure it was a girl now—sighed. Her bony shoulders gave a shrug from underneath the roomy sweatshirt, and she threw the hood back off her head.

It *was* a girl. Her hair was dark brown and very curly. Half of it was stuck in her hood and she had to pull hard to get it out. It stuck out in all directions after that, kind of like the arms of an octopus.

The skin on her hands and face was light brown, except for the very tip of her nose, which, as I already mentioned, was red. Also, a little bit peely.

She was a perfectly ordinary girl.

I don't know why I was disappointed. I don't know what I had been expecting.

"I would wear a hood too," Cici's voice floated up from the back of the room, "if I had hair like *that*. Yikes."

Muffled giggles exploded around the room, but Ms. Filch didn't appear to notice.

"There now, isn't that better?" she said, beaming down at the new girl. "Class, this is Sylvia Juarez. Sylvia—"

"Syl*vie*," the girl corrected Ms. Filch. "My name is *Sylvie*."

"*Sylvie* just moved here from New Mexico. What do you think of Portland so far, Sylvie?"

Sylvie glanced over at me. I expected her to look embarrassed because of Ms. Filch's questions and Cici's snarky comment. *I* certainly would have been. But instead, she just looked kind of bored.

She grinned slightly and rolled her eyes at me. As though the two of us were sharing some private joke. As if she wanted to say, *Isn't this stupid?*

Sylvie turned back to our teacher.

"It rains here a lot," she answered.

"Oh, well, you'll get used to it," Ms. Filch assured her, smiling kindly before she turned back to the front of the room. "If everyone will open their books to page twenty-four, we will continue our discussion of the first American colonies."

Sylvie scrunched down in her seat and pulled her hood back up so that it was halfway over her head. Probably not enough so that Ms. Filch would tell her to take it off again, but enough to hide at least most of her hair.

She caught me watching her and rolled her eyes again.

It was a friendly eye roll, just like the one before. I smiled in response. I couldn't help it. She had one of those faces you just wanted to smile at.

But there was still something weird about her.

I thought about it the whole time Ms. Filch droned on about Jamestown. It wasn't Sylvie's crazy hair. Or even her neon orange sweatshirt. I didn't care that she was from New Mexico or that she had a sunburned nose.

It was around the time that Ms. Filch started describing the Starving Time (in gruesome detail) that I figured it out.

Sylvie had definitely looked right at me, at least twice. And both times, she hadn't seemed the least bit surprised to find that she was sitting next to a boy who was part dinosaur.

Yeah, there was definitely something weird about the new girl.

For the second half of last year, at lunchtime, Elliot and I had sat at the long table by the door. Along with Mary and a few other kids from our class.

But now that I was part dinosaur, it was just the two of us. And we had had to move to the table closest to the bathroom. If we were demoted any further, we'd probably have to sit *in* the bathroom.

Elliot probably still could have sat at the table by the door, if he'd wanted to. Actually, I'm pretty sure he did want to. He only sat with me out of loyalty, the same way I had sat with him for the first half of last year, when nobody else would sit near "Gigantor."

It was nice of him. But I could tell that remaining friends with me was making him pretty miserable.

"It's only the second week," he said, smiling bravely as he unwrapped his sandwich. "Everyone will get over it. You'll see. Something else will come along."

"Like what?" I said, prying the lid off the jumbo-sized mixing bowl my mom had packed my salad into. "Something weirder than me? I doubt it."

Elliot's gaze flicked down to my tail, which had started twitching happily at the smell of my fresh greens. The tennis balls at the ends of my spikes made cheerful *bong, bong* sounds against the floor with every twitch.

Elliot shook his head sadly.

I shoved a giant forkful of lettuce into my mouth. I looked up just in time to be half blinded by a patch of neon orange.

Sylvie stood uncertainly in front of our table. She was holding a large, insulated lunch sack.

"Can I sit?" she asked, when neither Elliot nor I said anything.

I nodded, my mouth still full. Elliot cleared his throat.

"Sure," he said.

Under his breath, he mumbled, "*Why not? It can't get any worse.*"

Sylvie either didn't hear or didn't mind, because she smiled and set down her sack. Her hood was back up, and when she went to sit down, it fell forward so that it was almost impossible to see her face. She unzipped her sack and busied herself with setting out her lunch.

First, she removed a pink, disk-shaped tortilla warmer. Next came a tin-foil pie plate with a white lid. Sylvie peeled back the lid to reveal a pile of peppers, onions, and strips of chicken. They were so hot I could see the steam rising from them.

Then she took out small containers of salsa, cheese, and sour cream. Last was a medium-sized container of rice.

Elliot watched, fascinated.

"What *is* all of that?" he asked.

Sylvie surveyed the feast, wrinkled her peely nose, and then sat back in her chair without touching any of it.

"Chicken fajitas," she answered, sounding bored.

"For *lunch*?" I asked. It reminded me of the takeout my dad would sometimes pick up on his way home from work. But I would never get to take something so fancy to school with me. Not even back when I ate things like fajitas.

Elliot was looking down at his half-eaten sandwich with chagrin.

"My mom owns a restaurant," Sylvie explained. "These are just leftovers from the kitchen. Do you guys want any? We could trade."

I shook my head and pointed to my salad.

"I'm good," I said. "But thanks."

"I'll trade!" Elliot exclaimed.

"What d'you got?"

Sylvie leaned over to examine his lunch.

Other than the half-eaten sandwich, which I knew from experience was probably filled with sprouts and some sort of meat substitute,

Elliot had only some carrots, a container of hummus, and a cup of chocolate pudding.

"Not much," he admitted. "*My* mom is a health nut."

Sylvie pointed to the pudding.

"I'll trade you for that."

"OK," Elliot said, and quickly handed over the cup.

Sylvie shoved the fajita makings across the table at him.

"All of it?" Elliot asked uncertainly.

Sylvie nodded and opened the pudding.

"I'm sick of Mexican food," she explained. I found this kind of funny, considering that she probably was Mexican. At least, I thought she might be. It was hard to tell, considering most of her was hidden under the giant sweatshirt.

Sylvie took a bite of the pudding and immediately made a face.

"It's soy," Elliot explained. "My mom makes it herself."

He paused, a half-made fajita in one hand. Probably worried that Sylvie might be reconsidering their trade.

But Sylvie just set the pudding down, reached into the front pocket of her sweatshirt, and pulled out a handful of candy. She deposited it on the table and studied the pile carefully, finally selecting a banana Laffy Taffy.

She unwrapped the taffy, popped it into her mouth, and turned to me.

"So," she said. "You're part dinosaur. What's that like?"

"Pretty crappy," I admitted. It was sort of a weird question, but I didn't mind. It was nice that somebody was finally asking me, right to my face, instead of wondering behind my back.

Sylvie seemed surprised by my answer.

"Really? I think it's kind of cool."

I snorted.

"You don't have to live with it."

Sylvie nodded, her face serious, as she unwrapped a second Laffy Taffy. This one was pink and smelled like strawberry to my hyper-sensitive dino nose.

"That's true," she said. "I hadn't thought of it like that."

"Oh my GOD," Elliot broke in, taking a second bite of an overloaded fajita and causing sour cream to squirt out of the opposite end. He rolled his eyes in happiness, chewed, swallowed, and then added, "This is *ridiculous*. Your mom's restaurant must be *awesome*. Where is it? I'm going to eat there every day from now on."

"The one in Portland isn't open yet," Sylvie told him, with a slight smile. "Not until next week. But she and my dad own a couple of other ones, and they all do pretty well."

"Back in New Mexico?" I guessed, remembering Ms. Filch's introduction.

"There. And a couple of other places," Sylvie mumbled, rooting through her pile of candy.

"Your dad?" Elliot prompted her. When Sylvie didn't respond, he added, "Sorry, you made it sound like it was just your mom who owned the restaurant…"

"My parents are separated," Sylvie said, and her slight smile faded. "That's why my mom and I moved to Portland. But I'm probably not going to be here very long. I'm really supposed to be living with my dad. He's on a business trip right now, but he's coming to take me home with him as soon as he gets back."

"Won't your mom mind?" I asked her.

Sylvie shrugged.

"She only cares about the restaurant."

"Does your dad live around here?" Elliot asked.

Sylvie considered this.

"He lives a little bit outside of Portland," she answered finally.

Elliot nodded wisely.

"You'll probably have to change schools then. When you go to live with him, I mean. That sucks."

"Yeah," Sylvie agreed.

There was an uncomfortable silence after that, so I filled it with the only thing that came to mind.

"I used to like Mexican food," I said, feeling a little bit sorry for myself. "But ever since…this"—I gestured to my plates—"all I've really wanted to eat is salad. And fruit. Lots of fruit."

"*Stegosaurus* was an herbivore," Elliot explained, presumably for Sylvie's benefit.

"So you haven't always been part dinosaur?" she asked me. Without waiting for an answer, she picked up a Pixy Stix, tipped her head back, and dumped the entire contents into her mouth.

"Oh no, Sawyer was totally normal last year," Elliot answered, and then smiled an apology. "Sorry, man. You're still normal. I just mean—"

"No, he's not," Sylvie interrupted, through a mouthful of sugar.

I looked over at her, feeling surprised and hurt. So she *did* think it was weird. I guess I couldn't really blame her.

Sylvie shrugged unapologetically.

"Well, you're not. Normal, I mean. My dad always says that no one is normal. Not once you get to know them."

She smiled at me then, and there were sugar crystals stuck in her teeth.

"I guess you're right," I said, feeling a little bit less hurt than I had a moment ago. "But most people can hide their weirdness a little bit better than I can."

"Yeah, that's true."

Sylvie opened a tiny package of Twizzlers. She pulled them apart, one by one, and dangled them into her mouth like worms.

Elliot looked over at me. He had part of a red pepper dangling from his bottom lip, and his eyes were very clearly saying, *Is this girl for real?*

I shrugged.

Whether she was for real or not, Sylvie had definitely found her table.

The one closest to the bathroom. With us.

Ring Toss

Sylvie's arrival distracted Allan and his crew from the fact that there was a part-dinosaur in their midst for one entire day.

Once that day was over, their attention turned back to me. With a vengeance.

By the next morning, I could tell something strange was going on. Ms. Filch was telling us about the Plymouth Bay Colony, but I kept getting distracted by a strange sensation in my uppermost plates. Kind of like someone was tapping me on the shoulder, trying to get my attention.

But every time I turned around, no one was looking at me.

The third time it happened, I tried to whirl around really quickly, to catch the culprit. Unfortunately, I was packed so tightly in my chair that the only thing that actually whirled was my tail. It moved so quickly that one of my tennis balls hit Emma's chair leg and slid off the end of my spike. But my tail kept going, and the exposed spike sliced right through Brad Rivera's backpack.

Brad, a short, red-haired, immensely freckled kid who sat next to Emma, gaped down at his eviscerated backpack. Then he glared at me.

"Watch it, Butt Brain!" he exclaimed, then reached down to pick up the discarded tennis ball. He threw it at me, hard, so that it hit me squarely in the chest before I could catch it.

"Brad!" Ms. Filch admonished. "Apologize to Sawyer *this instant.*"

"Sorry, *Butt Brain,*" Brad muttered.

Instead of responding, I fumbled with the tennis ball, trying to keep it from rolling off my lap. Part of me couldn't really blame Brad for being startled. After all, if my spike had hit his leg instead of his backpack, it might have cut off his foot. What was I going to do if something like *that* ever happened?

I was going to have to try harder to avoid sudden movements.

Slowly, deliberately, I leaned down to screw the tennis ball back on its spike. As I did, Brad leaned his head down beside mine.

"You're going to pay for that, freak."

The weird sensations in my plates continued. But there was no way I was going to risk turning around again. So I just tried to ignore it.

My only hint as to what was going on was when I spotted something roll underneath my seat. I managed to trap it with my right foot. And when Ms. Filch wasn't looking, I reached down (carefully) to pick it up.

It was a yellow diving ring. The kind you find on the bottom of swimming pools.

This didn't make any sense to me until we were walking to lunch, and Elliot handed me three more rings: one red one and two blues.

"These were stuck on your plates," he explained. "Allan, Cici, and a few others were throwing them at you all morning."

My face burned as we entered the cafeteria and walked to our table.

"Why would they do that?" I asked, yawning. I had spent a long night on the Internet, searching for any hint of a cure for the dinosaur gene. I hadn't found a thing. So today I was both tired and grumpy.

"I'm pretty sure it's for points," Sylvie answered, appearing out of nowhere, dropping down into her seat and pushing a sheet of paper toward me. "I stole this out of Allan's desk just now."

NAME	RING COLOR	POINTS SCORED
Allan	Red	X (Tail)
Cici	Blue	X (Tail)
		XX (Upper Plate)
Brad	Yellow	
Ernie	Green	

A game. They had made a game out of me and my plates.

"Principal Mathis is going to kill them," Elliot predicted, unwrapping his sandwich. "Didn't they see what happened to Parker?"

"Who's Parker?" Sylvie asked, pulling a handful of candy out of her sweatshirt pocket. She was wearing the same orange sweatshirt she had worn the day before. But today, all of the candy in it appeared to be Tootsie Rolls of various colors. She laid them on the table in front of her and started unwrapping them.

"The kid who used to sit in your seat," Elliot answered, watching Sylvie with interest. Eventually, his attention wandered to her unopened lunch sack. "Are you going to eat your lunch? Want to trade again?"

Sylvie passed him the bag.

"Go for it. I don't need to trade. It's tamales today, by the way."

"Nice!" Elliot dove into the bag.

I motioned to the pile of naked Tootsie Rolls.

"Are you going to eat any of those?" I asked, honestly interested. I had never met anyone who was as weird about food as Sylvie.

"Eventually," she assured me. "Why do I have Parker's seat?"

"He got kicked out of school," Elliot told her, around a mouthful of tamale. "Principal Mathis caught him making fun of Sawyer, and we have a zero tolerance policy here."

Sylvie nodded, gathered up all of the Tootsie Rolls, and started squishing them into a giant ball between her hands.

"We should give the paper to Principal Mathis," she said finally, nodding to the score sheet in front of me. "It's evidence. Now she'll be able to kick out Allan and Cici. And the other two…"

"No," I said. Rule Number One, and all.

Elliot pried his eyes away from the sticky mess in Sylvie's hands and looked at me. There was a surprised look on his face.

"Why not?" he asked. "They're awful. Not just to you—I mean, *especially* to you—but they're mean to everybody! We'd all be better off without them here."

I knew he was thinking about last year, back when he had been their target.

"I'm not a tattletale," I explained.

"But—" Elliot started to argue with me, but he was cut off when Brad walked purposefully up to our table.

He veered slightly to the left as he approached us, as though he was headed toward the bathroom. But at the last second, he executed a wildly exaggerated fake trip. Stumbling over nothing, he flailed his arms and fell toward our table.

He caught himself on the edge with one hand. He used the other to knock my water bottle into my lap.

"Oops," he said loudly. "Sorry about that!" Quietly, he added, "You little dinosaur turd. Keep your tail to yourself!"

Brad continued on to the bathroom, pausing only to turn and throw a conspiratorial grin back to the table by the door. Allan, sitting at the head of the table, returned the grin and gave Brad a not so subtle thumbs up.

I used my one and only napkin to mop up the water in my lap. It was soaked instantly. Silently, Elliot and Sylvie both handed me theirs.

I blotted my damp lap with a sigh. For the rest of the day, it was going to look like I had peed my pants.

"You know," Sylvie said, tossing her Tootsie Roll ball back and forth between her hands, as though she was contemplating throwing it, "for a dinosaur, you don't have much of a backbone."

"Thanks for the support," I snapped. Suddenly all of the anger I had toward Brad was directed at Sylvie. Why had she decided to sit at our table if she was just going to make things worse?

"I'm sorry, but I'm just telling the truth," Sylvie said, not sounding sorry at all. "Sawyer, you've got to *do something* when that sort of thing happens. You have to stand up for yourself."

"What's he supposed to do?" Elliot demanded. "Stab Brad with his tail spikes? He'd just say that spilling the water had been an accident. And Sawyer would be the one who ended up in trouble."

I had been thinking the *exact* same thing. I'm pretty sure that's why Elliot and I are such good friends.

Sylvie, however, seemed to have her own way of thinking about things.

"I don't think you need to be that dramatic about it," she said. "Stabbing seems a little bit extreme."

"Then what?" I asked.

Sylvie shrugged and took a bite of her Tootsie Roll ball.

"We'll see," she said thoughtfully.

That night, I picked up my computer and pulled up my email.

Nothing. My grandfather had still not responded.

After that, I drifted off into an uneasy half sleep where I had mixed-up dreams about dinosaurs diving for rings in a really big pool.

Sylvie's swiping of the score sheet did not prevent the ring toss game from getting even more popular. Over the next couple of days, an increasingly diverse array of colored rings whizzed and rolled past me. So many, in fact, that Allan probably had to make a new score sheet anyway. Just to keep track of all the new players.

The game always got particularly intense during science class. The science lab had tables and stools instead of desks, which was both good and bad news for me. Good news because it meant my plates got a break from being squashed against the back of my chair. Bad news because my stool was in the front row of the classroom, and all my plates were exposed and vulnerable to everyone sitting behind me.

I was a sitting duck.

That afternoon, Dr. Cook was talking to us about the upcoming science fair. He was so excited that he was particularly distracted, and he turned his back on us frequently to write on the whiteboard at the front of the room.

Every time he did, it was game on. Every couple of minutes I felt another *thump* on my back. Or, when they missed (which was often), the *thump* was on my head, my stool, or even my tail.

"The science fair is the perfect opportunity for you to really get into the spirit of the scientific method," Dr. Cook explained, and turned to write "S-C-I-E-N-T-I-F-I-C M-E-T-H-O-D" on the board.

Thump.

"Let your curiosity run wild!"

Thump.

I tuned out Dr. Cook and thought about what Sylvie had said.

Thump.

It wasn't that I didn't *want* to stand up for myself. Of course I did. But what would I do? Stand up and yell at them to quit it? I could just *picture* the grin on Allan's face if I were to do that. For one thing, my yelling would not make them stop. And once I did that, they would know without a doubt that I knew what they were doing. They would know that I wanted to stop them, but couldn't.

Thump.

At least when I ignored them, I wasn't giving them the satisfaction. As long as I didn't acknowledge them, they wouldn't know that I cared.

Dr. Cook bent to retrieve something behind his desk. Whatever it was, he seemed to be having some trouble finding it because he disappeared from view for almost a full minute. This was the best opportunity any of the ring toss players were going to get, and they knew it.

Thump thump thump.

"Score!" I heard Allan stage whisper behind me.

I had just started to relax when I felt another ring hit me. Whoever had thrown it was a terrible shot. It hit the back of my head and then landed on the next lab table over, right in front of Sylvie, with a loud *THUD*.

Dr. Cook must have heard it, because his head of untidy gray hair suddenly popped up over the top of his desk.

Sylvie quickly grabbed the ring and pulled it underneath her desk. I was only barely able to see that it was purple.

"Everything all right?" Dr. Cook asked.

Purple? I didn't remember seeing a purple ring before. This must be a new player.

"Yes, Dr. Cook," we all chanted.

He nodded, only a bit suspiciously, and disappeared back behind his desk.

Sylvie turned around. She reached over Ernie, who sat directly behind her, and carefully handed the purple ring to Nora Phillips, two tables back.

"Here you go," she said.

"Uh, thanks."

When Nora reached up to grab the ring from Sylvie, I saw two other purple rings looped around her wrist. I seemed to recall that the rings usually came in packages of three.

Nora brushed one of her two blond braids over her shoulder and smiled at Sylvie. Sylvie smiled back, and then turned around in her seat without looking at me.

At least now I knew who the purple rings belonged to. But I was really more concerned with Sylvie's betrayal.

Maybe she didn't like sitting at our lunch table after all. Maybe a lack of backbone was a deal breaker for her, as far as friends were concerned. Maybe she had decided to use the ring toss game to get in good with the popular kids.

"Sorry about that, everyone," Dr. Cook said, emerging from behind his desk with a typical, three-paneled, foam core science project display. "Here we are. Now, this was one of the winning projects from last year's fair. As you can see, this student paid great attention to detail and made a nice use of color..."

I stared miserably at the table in front of me. I had *liked* Sylvie, right from the beginning. And not just because she smiled at me and said she thought my dinosaur plates were "cool." There had been something about her that I thought I recognized. She was weird, that was for sure. With her sweatshirt and her candy and all of that. But there was something about her that I thought I had understood. It was the same sort of something I felt around Elliot. I had hoped that the three of us could be friends.

Now I found myself wondering what color rings Sylvie would choose, once she officially joined the game. That is, if her name wasn't already on the score sheet.

I realized that everybody around me was pulling out their notebooks. Numbly, I did the same.

"The eight headings that you *must include* in your display are as follows," Dr. Cook was saying, writing on the board as he said them aloud. "Abstract. Question. Hypothesis. Background. Meth—"

"Ow!" came a voice behind me.

Dr. Cook turned away from the board. "Nora? Was that you? Is something wrong?"

"No, it's nothing. *OW!*"

Dr. Cook put down his dry erase marker and hurried to Nora's side. I turned on my stool to get a better view.

"What's going on, Nora?" Dr. Cook asked. He looked concerned.

"Nothing!" Nora smiled brightly. So brightly that she looked kind of insane.

Dr. Cook's concern converted to suspicion, faster than water converts to hydrogen and oxygen.

"Let me see your hands," he commanded.

Nora's smile faded. Her hands were hidden beneath her desk, and she made no movement to bring them out.

"I'm really fine now," she told Dr. Cook. "All better."

"Hands, Nora. *Now.*"

Nora cast a helpless glance around the room, and then put both hands on the desk in front of her.

There were still two purple diving rings around her right wrist. The third was clenched in her right fist.

Dr. Cook put out his hand.

"Give those to me,"

"I *can't*," Nora said miserably, tears forming in her eyes. "It's *stuck!*"

Dr. Cook took Nora's wrist and tried to pull the ring out of her hand.

"Ow!" Nora howled.

"It *is* stuck," Dr. Cook said incredulously, examining Nora's hands more gently.

Suddenly, as though he was emerging from a dream, Dr. Cook's head snapped up. His eyes went to the floor and traveled up the trail of multicolored diving rings that led to my lab table.

"Ernie," Dr. Cook said quietly. "Please go get Principal Mathis. Tell her she is needed here immediately."

"Yes, sir!" Ernie, eager to obey as always, ran for the door.

Dr. Cook returned to the front of the room. He leaned against his desk and crossed his arms, watching us like a hawk.

"The rest of you will sit quietly until Principal Mathis arrives. Do you understand?"

We all nodded.

"Hands on your desks," he ordered.

We all hastened to obey. I had never heard Dr. Cook sound so severe. The look on his face was *scary*. Even to me. And I was pretty sure that I wasn't the one in trouble.

"No moving," he warned us. "Not one muscle."

We sat in total silence.

I'm not sure how long we would have stayed like that. At some point, somebody, probably Allan, would have gotten over their fear enough to crack a joke or scratch an itch or something. That would have broken the spell. But it wasn't very long at all before I heard the classroom door open behind us and the sound of Principal Mathis's heels squeaking on the tile as she walked to the front of the room.

Dr. Cook and Principal Mathis had a short, whispered conference that even I, in the front row, could not hear. As Dr. Cook talked, I saw Principal Mathis's eyes move from Allan, to me, and back to Allan again.

Finally, Principal Mathis faced us and cleared her throat.

"Please raise your hand if there are any diving rings, of any color, in your possession."

I sneaked a look behind me. Only Nora was raising her hand, and that was probably only because her fingers were still clenched around the purple ring. There was really no point in her trying to pretend she was innocent, like everyone else was doing.

Principal Mathis was undaunted.

"I want you all to empty your desks. And your pockets. And

your backpacks. Put everything on top of the table in front of you. Right now."

Nobody said anything, but the room was suddenly full of scuffling noises as everybody piled their belongings in front of them.

I tried to catch Sylvie's eye as I unzipped my backpack, but she didn't look at me. She had already stacked her books neatly on her lab table and was now building a tower of Kit Kats beside them.

Principal Mathis walked up and down the aisles, pausing beside each student to poke through their stuff. Whenever she found a diving ring, she leaned down and whispered in that student's ear. Afterward, that student got up and stood in a perfect line in the back of the room.

First it was Gary Simmons. Then Mary Bishop. Then Brad. Then, no surprise, it was Nora. And finally, a girl named Vivian Cho. Principal Mathis lined up all five of them beside the classroom door.

Allan and Cici were not among those rounded up, even though Principal Mathis spent longer at Allan's table than at anyone else's.

"Thank you, Dr. Cook," Principal Mathis said finally. "So sorry to disturb your class."

She left the room. The line of ring-tossers left with her.

Dr. Cook cleared his throat and returned to the board.

"Where were we? Oh yes. Method. Procedure. Results. And Conclusion. Each of these headings deserves a separate space on your project display…"

Next to me, Sylvie made a small movement.

She stuck her hand down by her leg and opened her fingers slightly, so that I could see what she was holding.

It was a tiny tube of superglue.

9

Layups/Standing Up

At first, I wondered how Allan and Cici had avoided being caught up in what came to be known as "the Great Purge." But the answer soon became clear.

At lunchtime immediately following that epic morning in the science lab, Elliot pulled six rings off my plates, three red and three yellow. On the scorecard Sylvie had stolen, those were Allan's and Cici's colors.

They had gotten so good at the game, they hadn't had any rings left to bust them.

After the Great Purge, nobody ever played the ring toss game again. But that didn't mean everyone left me in peace. The next day, Jeremy Harris tripped me on the way to the computer lab. And during lunch, I discovered that someone had written "DINO DORK" with a purple felt-tip marker on all of my tennis balls.

That afternoon, when Principal Mathis arrived to take Jeremy away, she also searched Emma's desk. I was shocked when she discovered the purple marker.

"Vivian was my best friend," Emma hissed at me, as she gathered up her Hello Kitty backpack.

I watched sadly as Emma's pink Converse disappeared out the door, right behind Jeremy and Principal Mathis. I hadn't known Jeremy at all. Actually, I had always assumed he was kind of strange because he wore overalls all the time. But I had thought Emma was one of the nice ones.

As I gazed after Emma, I caught Allan glaring at me. As though this was all my fault. He sat two rows behind me and slightly to the left.

I didn't like that he sat behind me. It made it far too easy for him to watch me. Whereas, if I wanted to look at him, I had to go through the uncomfortable, slow process of twisting around and smashing all my plates against the back of the chair.

I had a feeling Allan was planning his next move. But I didn't get to find out what it was until gym, a few days after the Great Purge.

Our basketball unit had started early this year. Elliot was, of course, thrilled. But I was miserable. If you ever try dribbling a basketball with a long tail trailing behind you, you'll understand why.

That day, we were supposed to be learning layups. Coach Carpenter demonstrated the concept (which, it was obvious to me, I would never come close to achieving) and split us into groups beneath the gym's four basketball hoops to practice.

I waited glumly for my turn to come. When I was almost at the front of the line, I saw Cici attempt a layup on the next hoop over. She tripped, fell on her face, and lay sprawled out on the gym floor, moaning.

Even from a distance, it looked fake. So I wasn't exactly surprised when, as soon as Coach Carpenter ran to her aid, Allan appeared in front of me.

He stood with his back to Cici and the coach and used his enormous head to cut me off from everyone else in the gym.

"Time for a chat, Butt Brain," Allan said, reaching into his pocket and pulling out half of a bologna sandwich.

He must have been doing it just to bug me. I mean, who else brings a sandwich to gym? I tried not to make a face as he raised it to his lips and bit off most of it in just one bite.

Allan watched me carefully as he chewed. He did it with his mouth open, and I could see shreds of bologna dangling from his teeth.

The smell of meat was nauseating. The whole thing made my stomach lurch. I didn't say anything because I didn't trust myself not to hurl. But I didn't let myself look away until he finished the sandwich with a second smaller bite and stuffed the empty baggy back into his shorts pocket.

"What happened to Parker?" he asked me, as he wiped his mouth. "And the other kids who got kicked out?"

"What do you mean?" I asked. I tried to sound casual, even though my mind was working overtime, trying to figure out what he was getting at.

"You heard me," he said, crossing his arms. "*Where* is Parker?"

"How should I know? He got kicked out of school. I haven't seen him since that day in the computer lab."

"Neither have I," Allan said icily. "Neither has *anyone*. His phone's been shut off, and he's not at his house. And Cici says it's the same with Nora and Vivian and all of the other kids too."

I frowned. It had never really occurred to me to wonder about Parker, or any of the other kids Principal Mathis had thrown out of school. I just assumed they'd had to enroll in the other public school, across town. Frankly, I had just been glad they were no longer around to torture me.

"It's not my problem," I told Allan.

"It is now," he informed me.

Allan swiveled his big head and glanced over his shoulder, to where Coach Carpenter was still bent over a prostrate Cici. The rest of our class was standing around, bored, waiting for the signal to return to layup practice. Elliot and Sylvie were among them, both watching me with worried eyes.

"Parker was my friend," Allan said, turning his head back to me. He took a step forward so that he was right in front of my face. "*What did you do to him?*"

I could smell the remnants of his sandwich on his breath. But I didn't become nauseated this time. Instead, I felt my entire body tense. My tail gave a warning twitch. Suddenly, I had a powerful urge to whirl around and whack Allan right in the face with the ends of my spikes.

There were only two problems with this:

1. The tennis balls probably would have made my tail just bounce off his cheekbones, instead of ripping his face to shreds.

2. That definitely would have been a violation of the school's code of conduct, not to mention my promise to Principal Mathis.

So instead, I looked Allan right in the eye. He was wearing his normal, annoyed expression. His thick eyebrows were knitted together in the very center of his ugly face. There was anger in his eyes, as usual, but there was something questioning there too.

He really does want to know where Parker is. He thinks I know something.

I decided to use that to my advantage.

I leaned even closer to Allan so that our faces were practically touching.

"Parker messed with me," I told him, in what I hoped was a menacing tone. "Don't make the same mistake."

Allan's eyes narrowed. I did not back down, although a large portion of my brain had already started to rethink the tough guy strategy.

Luckily, Coach Carpenter came to my rescue. Sort of.

"Back to business, everyone," his voice boomed. "And for heaven's sake, pay attention to where you put your feet. I don't have time to fill out any more accident reports today, OK?"

Allan and I continued to stand there, eyes locked, until Allan finally blinked.

"This isn't over," he informed me.

"Probably not," I agreed.

Allan turned and went to the back of the nearest layup line.

I stayed where I was until my shaking subsided enough for me to be able to walk to a line on the other side of the gym from Allan's.

I had done it. I had stood up for myself.

Sylvie was right. It felt good. I didn't feel like I had been stomped on and gotten the wind knocked out of me. Which is how I normally felt after an encounter with Allan. Instead, I felt full of energy. Like I might actually be able to do a layup without being weighed down by my plates and without tripping on my tail.

But I still couldn't help being the tiniest bit curious about what had really happened to Parker. And all the rest of the ring-toss kids who had been kicked out.

Later that day, after proving to everyone in gym class that my new-found confidence in my layup abilities was *entirely* in my head, I told Elliot and Sylvie what Allan had told me about Parker and the other kids who had been expelled.

"So they're just…gone?" Elliot asked.

I shrugged.

"I guess so. I don't know why Allan would lie about it."

"Ohhhh, intrigue!" Sylvie pulled her hood back a fraction of an inch. Her eyes were sparkling with excitement.

"It's not like they could all just *disappear,*" Elliot said. "That's crazy. We would have heard something about it."

"We could check their houses," Sylvie suggested. "It shouldn't be too hard to figure out where they all live. It must be nearby, right?"

I nodded. "Parker lives two streets away from me."

Sylvie smiled and rubbed her hands together.

"I guess we know what we're doing after school today!"

"No way." Elliot shook his head. "It's not like we're friends with Parker. We can't just show up at his house."

"We can if he doesn't know that we're there," Sylvie said, winking in Elliot's direction.

Elliot shook his head.

"This is a bad idea," he said, to no one in particular.

Bad idea or not, Sylvie could not be talked out of it. As soon as school was out for the day, the three of us walked to Parker's house.

We did our best to be stealthy. But let's face it, it's kind of hard to sneak up on someone when your group is made up of a part-dinosaur, a really tall kid, and a girl in a bright orange sweatshirt.

"We're like the worst spies ever," Elliot complained, picking the thoughts right out of my brain.

"Shhhh." Sylvie put a finger to her lips and ducked behind an oversized plant. She nodded to the house I had directed us to.

"You're sure that's it?" she whispered.

I nodded. I walked by Parker's house almost every day, but I had only actually been inside of it once. For a birthday party. Two years ago. When Parker's parents had forced him to invite everybody in the class, including me and Elliot. I remembered the red and blue stained glass parrot on their front door. Parker's parents were really into bird-watching or something.

I could see the bird through the branches of the plant we were hiding behind. Sylvie motioned for Elliot and me to stay put. Then she crawled on her hands and knees to peek her head around the side of the foliage.

Elliot shifted his long legs uncomfortably on the ground beside me. It wasn't actually raining (which was kind of miraculous, since it was afternoon in Portland), but the ground was still wet and slightly muddy from that morning's rain. We were all going to have wet butts after this. Mom was probably going to make me hose off my tail before she allowed me in my house.

Sylvie crawled back around to us.

"There's a light in the front hall," she reported. "That means someone must be home."

"See? Allan doesn't know what he's talking about," Elliot scoffed. "Can we go home now?"

"We haven't seen Parker yet," Sylvie reminded him. "Which room is his?"

Elliot looked over at me, and we both shrugged.

Sylvie gave us an exasperated look.

"We've only been here once," I reminded her. "And the party was mostly in the backyard."

"Fine," Sylvie said, and thought for a moment. "We'll have to sneak around the side of the house then and look in some windows. It shouldn't take us long to find his room."

To me, that sounded like an excellent way to get caught. Why was Sylvie so determined to see Parker? Perhaps she felt some sort of kinship with the kid whose desk she now sat in? I looked over at Elliot. From his face, I could tell he felt the same way I did. But since neither of us had the energy to argue with Sylvie, we got up off the muddy ground and followed her around the bush.

We were halfway up Parker's driveway when the garage door started to go up.

Sylvie motioned us frantically back to the bush. She and Elliot both scrambled back down the driveway and dove to safety.

I got as far as the edge of the driveway before something suddenly jerked me backward. I looked behind me.

One of my tail spikes had lost its tennis ball and was now stuck in a flowerbed. I reached back and tried to jerk my tail free, but the spike was buried too deep in the mud and wouldn't budge.

The garage door was now a quarter of the way up, and I thought I could hear somebody talking.

I turned around and tried to reach the end of my tail, so that I could dig it free. But my tail did not want to bend that way. I heard a pop, and I bit my lip to keep from yelling as I felt a sharp stab of pain, just above my spikes.

A small flash of orange appeared beside me and pulled my spike free. The yank sent another stab of pain racing up my tail, but I ignored it and followed Sylvie back to the safety of the bush.

I cradled my aching tail in my hands as we peered through the leaves to see if we had been caught.

A tall woman wearing shorts and tennis shoes walked out of the open garage. She was carrying a large garbage bag in one hand and holding a cell phone to her ear with the other.

"It's been difficult, of course," she was saying as she walked to the end of the driveway. "We miss him terribly. But we're managing."

Sylvie looked at me questioningly. I mouthed, *Parker's mom.*

The three of us crouched down even farther and did our best to be invisible. But Mrs. Douglas appeared oblivious to our presence, even when she paused at the end of the driveway, less than an arm's length away from us, on the other side of the plant.

"I finally got started on his room today," she said into the phone. "You wouldn't *believe* the clutter. It's going to take me days to clean it out!"

She swung the garbage bag onto the curb and turned, walking back into the garage. The three of us sat in silence as the garage door shuddered and slowly rolled back down.

Elliot and I stared at each other. Sylvie reached around the bush and dragged the garbage bag into her lap.

"She was talking about Parker, wasn't she?" Elliot said finally.

Instead of responding, Sylvie started picking at the knot on the top of the bag.

"I think so," I replied, the pain in my tail momentarily forgotten as I struggled to make sense of Mrs. Douglas's words.

It's been difficult... We miss him...

Those aren't the sorts of things you say about someone who has been safely enrolled in the school across town. Those are the kind of things you say when somebody has—

No, I told myself. *Don't even think it.*

"He can't be *dead*," Elliot whispered, stealing my thoughts again. "What could have happened?"

Sylvie gave up on the knot and ripped a hole in the side of the garbage bag, spilling the contents onto the muddy ground in front of her.

Clothes.

A wadded-up assortment of shirts, jeans, and track pants fell out of the bag. I spotted a familiar shade of red and pulled it out of the pile.

I shuddered as I recognized the sneering face of the Angry Bird.

The last time I had seen that shirt, Parker had been wearing it. And leading half of our computer class in the Butt Brain chorus.

I reached over and dug through the rest of the clothes, looking for holes. Stains. Rips. Anything that would explain why Mrs. Douglas would throw them away.

But there was nothing. The clothes were all perfectly ready to be worn. There was no reason to throw them away.

Unless, of course, there was no longer someone to wear them.

10

Do Stegosauruses Like Salsa?

That evening, my tail wouldn't stop hurting. So Mom took me to the vet.

The. *Vet.*

When I asked her why we weren't going to see my regular pediatrician, Dr. Bakker, my mom turned to me in exasperation.

"And just how many broken tails do you think Dr. Bakker has ever seen?" she demanded.

I guess she had a point.

But still. The *vet?*

Dr. Gilmore, whom I had last seen when we brought Fanny in to be spayed, saw me right away. She bumped me to the front of the line, ahead of a golden retriever who had bitten through his stitches and a Pekingese with an ear infection. After a quick X-ray, she diagnosed me with a sprained tail and sent me home with an anti-inflammatory and orders to ice the injured area.

My dignity was still smarting the next day, but my tail felt much better. And after school, Sylvie invited Elliot and me to visit her mother's new restaurant. My mom seemed unusually enthusiastic about my going. Probably because the restaurant was on the edge of downtown, quite a long walk away, and Dr. Gilmore had told her that exercise would help my tail heal properly.

The restaurant's front door was papered shut. There was a large banner draped over the front of the building, which read "COMING SOON—MAMA JUAREZ'S CUCINA." Over the door was a drawing of a smiling woman with Sylvie's hair and milk-chocolaty brown skin, offering a plate of tortillas to the passersby.

Sylvie led us in through a door in the back. Inside, several dozen tables were shoved together in the center of a large dining room, and four men on ladders were painting the walls bright orange.

"*Hola, mi hija!*" came a loud voice with a heavy accent.

I was enveloped in a big, squishy hug (along with Elliot and Sylvie) before I could see where the voice was coming from. When I could breathe again, I noticed that the hugger bore a striking resemblance to the woman whose picture was above the door, except that her smile was even brighter in person.

"Sit, sit!" she commanded, steering all three of us to one of the tables. "I'm so glad you've brought me some taste testers!"

"Some *what*?" Elliot asked, as four waiters appeared, each carrying a tray so heavily laden with food that the plastic was groaning with the weight. They spread the plates out on the table in front of us and then disappeared back into the kitchen.

Elliot sat obediently and grabbed a fork.

"Mo-*om*," Sylvie complained, scowling down at the table. There was easily enough food there for ten people.

"Shush." Mrs. Juarez kissed the top of her head. "You know it's been a long time since I've done straight Mexican food. We're finalizing the menu today, and I need opinions. Start with the tamales."

"Yes, ma'am," said Elliot, who was already halfway through with the plate in front of him.

Mrs. Juarez beamed at him. Elliot swallowed and seemingly remembered his manners.

"I'm Elliot," he said, sticking his hand out across a plate of enchiladas. Mrs. Juarez shook it.

"It's a pleasure to meet you, Elliot," she said, and then turned to me. "And you must be Sawyer?"

I shook her hand as well.

"That is a lovely tail you have there, Sawyer," Mrs. Juarez complimented me. "Don't you worry. I have a big salad coming for you. Do you like salsa?"

I considered this for a moment.

"I'm not sure," I said finally. "I don't think I've tried any since this summer."

She gave my shoulder a squeeze.

"I'll bring you out some, just in case you want to spice up your greens a bit."

"*All right,* Mom," Sylvie said pointedly, nudging a plate of chile rellenos to one side, to clear a spot for her notebook. "We'll try all of the food, OK?"

"*OK*, Sylvie," Mrs. Juarez said, in the exact same tone of voice.

Then she narrowed her eyes suspiciously at her daughter. "Empty your pockets."

"What do you mean?" Sylvie asked. Her face was suddenly a mask of wide-eyed innocence. The expression looked really weird on her.

"You know what I mean." Mrs. Juarez tapped a foot impatiently and held out a hand, palm up. "Pockets. Now."

Sylvie's innocent face melted, replaced by an annoyed scowl. Sighing, she dug into the front pocket of her sweatshirt and deposited two handfuls of candy corn into her mom's hand.

"*Sylvia*," Mrs. Juarez scolded, shaking her head at the candy. "You *know* what your father thinks about this."

"Dad's not here," Sylvie said quietly.

Mrs. Juarez started to say something and then stopped. Instead, she reached out and patted her daughter's head through her orange hoodie.

"I'm sure you've had enough sugar for the day," she said finally. "Time for some real food. Pop your head in the kitchen when you're ready to leave, OK? I'll give everybody a ride home."

"OK," Sylvie said, scowling at a bowl of chips.

Mrs. Juarez disappeared around a corner.

I sat down and took a sip of water while I studied Sylvie. She was still staring at the chips.

Sylvie's mom wasn't what I had pictured at all. From Sylvie's description, I had expected a mean woman who cared only about her restaurant. The real Mrs. Juarez hadn't seemed like that at all. What was Sylvie's problem?

I looked at Elliot across the table. He was chewing. Chewing and looking worriedly at Sylvie.

"So…your dad doesn't let you eat candy?" I ventured.

Sylvie looked up at me. For a moment, her eyes looked filled with hurt. I was just starting to get seriously concerned that she was about to cry when she blinked. And suddenly she was back to normal again.

"Dad has a thing about sugar," she said, reaching for a chip.

"And he's still on his business trip?" I prodded.

"Yep," Sylvie said flatly. Swallowing her chip, she opened her notebook and held a pen poised over the empty first page. "Focus, boys. We're here to work."

"Oh, sorry, yeah," Elliot said, pushing some enchiladas aside to grab another plate. "Let's try this one next. What is this? Then we can start on the—"

"No," Sylvie snapped at him. "We're not here to talk about food. We're here to talk about what is happening at our school."

"Oh." Elliot looked disappointed.

"Here is what we know," Sylvie said, leaning forward importantly. "Eight kids have been kicked out of school—"

"Ten," I interrupted. Justin Thomas and Gabrielle Clark had been sent to Principal Mathis's office that morning, after they both yelled "feeding time" and threw sandwich meat at me. I could only assume that had been Allan's idea.

"OK, ten," Sylvie amended, writing all of the names down in her notebook. "Ten kids have been expelled, and no one has heard from them since. We have visual confirmation that at least one of them is no longer living—"

"Now hold on—" Elliot interrupted.

"In his *house*," Sylvie added, interrupting him back. "No longer living *in his house*. Under suspicious circumstances that would lead a reasonable person to believe that something out of the ordinary has happened to him."

"That sounds about right," I agreed, as Mrs. Juarez returned holding a large bowl of salad.

I winced as my injured tail thumped with involuntary delight.

Mrs. Juarez placed the salad in front of me, along with two other smaller dishes.

"This one is salsa," she said, pointing to the first one, which was full of chunky bits of tomato and onion. "And this one," she said, pointing to the second one, a rich-looking brown sauce, "is molé."

"Molé?" Elliot asked, his mouth full again. "What is that?"

"A Mexican sauce, made from chilies, spices, nuts, chocolate, and a few other things," Mrs. Juarez answered.

"Chocolate?" Elliot exclaimed. "That's awesome!"

"You can't taste it," Sylvie said sulkily.

Mrs. Juarez frowned at her daughter.

"You can if you're paying attention, Sylvie. Let your friends make up their own minds."

Mrs. Juarez squeezed my shoulder as she straightened up.

"I thought it might go nicely with your salad, Sawyer. You must get tired of plain greens all of the time. And, Elliot, the same sauce is on the molé poblano. That's the dish on your left."

"Cool!" Elliot said, exchanging his scraped-clean plate for the one Mrs. Juarez had pointed out. It was a giant stuffed green pepper drizzled with the brown mystery sauce.

"Thanks," I said, and gave my small dish of molé an experimental sniff. It smelled…warm. Which sounds weird, but it really did. Warm, like spices and nuts. I poured it over the top of my salad.

Mrs. Juarez returned to the kitchen, and we returned to our conversation.

"I *really* don't think that Parker is dead," Elliot offered, as he disemboweled the poblano with a knife. "If anything like that had happened to him, or to any of the others, we would have heard about it. Remember Gwen Carmichael?"

I nodded, as Sylvie frowned.

"Who is Gwen Carmichael?"

"A sixth grader who died in a car accident last year," I explained, as I took a bite of the molé-covered salad. It *was* spicy. Spicy enough that I felt my eyebrows shoot up in surprise as soon as it hit my tongue. Somewhere behind the spice, I thought I could also taste the chocolate. But maybe that was just my imagination. I swallowed before I continued.

"We basically didn't even have school for two weeks after she died. We had special assemblies and meetings with crisis counselors, and we all had to make these fake roses out of tissue paper for her funeral. Stuff like that. It was all any of the teachers talked about for weeks."

"And Gwen wasn't even in our grade," Elliot pointed out. "There's no way ten kids *in our class* have died and we haven't heard anything about it."

Sylvie nodded and wrote *Gwen Carmichael* in block letters in her notebook.

"So the school made a big deal about a student dying," she

summed up. "But they haven't done anything about the ten kids who got kicked out. Interesting."

"Which means they didn't die," Elliot surmised, as he scraped a bit of dribbled sauce off his black Oregon State Beavers jersey.

"*Or* it means somebody is covering it up," Sylvie countered.

"Covering what up?" I asked, coughing a little bit after my second bite of molé. This was definitely a sauce that fought back when you ate it. But I didn't mind. Mrs. Juarez was right. I *had* been getting a little bit tired of plain veggies all of the time.

"Whatever happened to them," Sylvie answered. "I'm not saying they all *died*. But Parker's mom said she missed him. And if he's still alive, he's definitely somewhere where he doesn't need any of his clothes. That's weird. Can we all agree that that's weird?"

"It's weird," Elliot agreed. "But what can we do about it?"

"We can find out what's going on," Sylvie said. Her expression was so determined that I could tell Elliot and I were already on board with her plan, whatever it was, whether we liked it or not.

"Who do you think is covering it up?" I asked. "And why?"

Sylvie tapped her pen against her chin.

"I'm not sure about the *why*," she admitted. "But I think that part will be obvious, once we figure out the *who*."

"Then *who* is covering this up?" I asked again. "And do we even know what *this* is?"

"*This* is a confusing conversation," Elliot muttered, chewing.

"The obvious *who* is Principal Mathis," Sylvie said. "She's the one who is kicking all these kids out in the first place, right?"

"She's the principal. It's kind of her job," I pointed out. I suddenly felt defensive on Principal Mathis's behalf. She was, after all, going to a lot of trouble to defend me against the kids who were making my life miserable.

"Yeah, but if anyone knows what's happening to them, it's got to be Principal Mathis," Elliot agreed. "Even if she's not the one doing it, principals know those kinds of things, right? They have files and stuff?"

"We need to find a way to sneak into her office," Sylvie decided.

"What!" I exclaimed. "Why can't we just ask her?"

Sylvie and Elliot exchanged *that's stupid* looks.

"If she's hiding something, she's not just going to come out and tell us what it is," Sylvie informed me.

"We're just kids," Elliot reminded me. "I doubt she'd talk to us about other students. Even if she's *not* hiding anything."

"I vote that we sneak into her office and see what we can find," Sylvie said.

"I vote that too," Elliot agreed, and shoveled a spoonful of rice into his mouth.

I frowned. Somehow, the two of them had managed to get on the same page. But they had left me a few pages behind.

Still, I found myself nodding in agreement. Sometimes, especially when you're part dinosaur, it's easier to just go along with the crowd.

I grabbed a napkin to dab my watering eyes. I had eaten my entire salad. And now it felt like the molé was trying to escape through my eyeballs. Also through my nose, which had started running.

All of a sudden I felt a sneeze coming on. I could tell it was going to be massive, but even I wasn't prepared for how loud it was when it finally came.

"AAAAAACCCCCCHHHHHOOOOOOOOOOO!"

Sylvie and Elliot both jumped. The guy at the top of the ladder nearest us jumped, too, and glared down at us.

"Wow!" Elliot exclaimed. "That was one big dinosaur sneeze!"

I shrugged and wiped my nose. I felt better. Like when a cold you've had for a long time finally goes away. Kind of cleaned out. Maybe I should eat spicy food more often.

11

That Stupid T. Rex from Jersey

The next morning, during computer class, Mr. Broome woke up for long enough to saddle us all with a boring spreadsheet assignment, then promptly went back to sleep at his desk. Almost immediately, people started gathering around Allan's computer, just the way they had on the second day of school.

And once again, Allan's big head was blocking the screen so I couldn't see what they were looking at.

"Uh-oh," I heard Sylvie say.

She had taken the computer next to mine. Elliot was on the other side of her, and she had just angled her screen to show Elliot something.

I got a sinking feeling in my stomach.

"What?" I asked.

Sylvie moved her screen so that I could see it too.

It was the *Portland Daily News* website. And the top headline was: *Dinosaur Hybrid Goes Prehistoric, Bites Classmate*

My first reaction was a strange mixture of guilt and confusion. Had I bitten someone and somehow forgotten about it? Who had I bitten? Had I hurt them? My teeth were still quite human, so I couldn't have done any more damage to them than an ordinary human…

But then I remembered Amalgam Labs, and how I wasn't the only dinosaur hybrid in the world.

"It was in New Jersey," Sylvie reported, scanning the article. "A T. rex hybrid. He bit another kid in the middle of a soccer game."

"Well, that's a relief," I joked. "I only bite people over volley-ball disputes."

Sylvie and Elliot both snickered, but the half dozen kids who were gathered around Allan's computer all turned around and stared at me, openmouthed.

I gulped. I hadn't realized they would take this so seriously.

"I'm kidding," I told them all. "I don't bite people."

"This kid didn't either," Allan said, pointing at his computer screen. They had also been reading the article. "Until he *did*."

"That kid is a T. rex," Elliot pointed out. "A meat eater."

"What does that have to do with anything?" Cici demanded. As usual, she was right next to Allan, backing him up. I wondered if she ever used her brain at all or if she just let Allan do all the thinking for the pair of them. Which didn't seem like the best plan to me, considering how stupid Allan was.

"Stegosauruses are herbivores. They eat plants." Elliot explained. Then, with exaggerated patience, he added, "That means that Sawyer is more likely to attack the fern in the back of the classroom than you."

"Doubtful. I'm pretty sure it's plastic," I muttered.

But nobody was listening to me.

"A dinosaur is a dinosaur," Cici sniffed. "Who cares if he *looks* like *Stegosaurus*? He might have the appetite of *T. rex*. We won't know until he starts eating us."

"The article says the kid in New Jersey didn't even need stitches," Sylvie pointed out. "He wasn't *eaten*."

"Oh sure." Allan rolled his eyes. "That school is probably just protecting their dino boy. The same way this school protects Sawyer."

I opened my mouth to say something in response. I'm not sure exactly what. But before I could say anything, Allan just gave an angry grunt and turned his back on me.

"Whatever." Sylvie dismissed the whole thing with a wave of her hand. "Maybe now they'll leave you alone. Try gnashing your teeth at them every now and then. That might help."

"Sure," I said, frowning at my computer screen. I had no intention of gnashing my teeth at anybody. But maybe Sylvie was right. Maybe this T. rex kid gnawing on somebody's arm in New Jersey would turn out to be the best thing that had ever happened to me.

It did not turn out to be the best thing that had ever happened to me.

For one thing, the staring started again. There had been a lot of staring at the beginning of the year, on the playground and in the halls. It had never really gone away completely, but people at our school had gotten somewhat used to having a part-dinosaur in their midst. To the point where I could walk the halls without people gasping in surprise or stopping whatever they were doing to gape at me.

But now, the gaping was back.

Before, I had just been kind of an oddity. My plates were pretty harmless looking, and my tail spikes were always tennis-balled, so I don't think it had occurred to anyone to be scared of me.

Until now.

Now everyone watched me with a mixture of worry and curiosity, as though I was just a heartbeat away from randomly attacking someone in the hallway.

I was pretty sure that not a single one of them had bothered to read past the headline to find out what had really happened. I, however, had spent the remainder of computer class reading every article I could find on the situation. And as far as I could tell, the T. rex hybrid (a third grader) had bitten a sixth grader on the arm after the sixth grader attacked him for no reason. A school nurse treated the sixth grader's arm with disinfectant and two Band-Aids, while the hybrid had landed in the hospital with a broken nose. (Er, snout? The articles weren't too clear on the proper terminology for a T. rex nasal appendage.)

But all anybody at our school cared about was that a dinosaur hybrid had bitten someone. The reasons and circumstances behind the bite didn't matter at all.

What mattered was when *I* was going to bite someone. And from the looks I was getting, it was clear that the kids at my school had decided it was only a matter of time before I chose my first victim.

At lunch that day, there seemed to be more space than usual between our table and the rest of the room. We were the same distance from the bathroom as before, so I could only assume that other kids had moved their tables away from us.

On the off chance that I decided to go on a biting frenzy, I suppose.

The only person who didn't keep his distance from me was the only person I may have actually been inclined to bite. If I had given the matter any serious thought. Which, for the record, I had not.

Allan approached our table

"You really think you're fooling anybody with that salad, Butt Brain?"

He gestured angrily to my mixing bowl.

I swallowed a bite of tomato and glared up at him.

"What do you want, Allan?" I asked, trying to sound bored.

He put both his hands on the table and leaned down over me. He kept a smile on his face so the lunch monitor would think it was just a friendly chat. But his voice was shaking with rage as he whispered into my ear.

"I know you're eating them."

"Eating who?" I asked, not bothering to whisper back.

"The kids who got kicked out," Allan said, continuing to whisper. "That's why no one has heard anything from them."

His voice had been loud enough for Elliot and Sylvie to hear. I looked over at them. Elliot's mouth dropped open.

Sylvie started giggling.

Allan turned to her, his huge eyebrows squished together in a frown.

"Shut up, Fence Jumper," he commanded. Smiling even brighter, for the lunch monitor, he raised his voice to her. "I'll bet that's why you hide under that stupid hood all the time, isn't it? You don't want anyone to recognize you? Don't want us to find out your parents are illegal aliens?"

Sylvie only laughed harder. So hard, I was pretty sure we were all in real danger of having Pixy Stix dust sprayed out of her nose at us.

But I didn't think it was funny. I glared at Allan.

"Don't talk to her like that," I said, hoping I sounded threatening.

"I didn't come over here to talk to her," he said dangerously. "I just want you to know that I *know*. I know you're eating them."

"That's crazy," I told him. "You're *crazy*. Why would I eat anybody?"

"Because you're a monster," Allan told me. "Just like that kid in Jersey. I knew from the very beginning that it was only a matter of time before you went all dinosaur-psycho on us."

"Shut up," I muttered. I was so angry my hands were shaking, but I hid them under the table so Allan wouldn't see.

"Make me," Allan suggested.

My hands started to shake harder. It wasn't because I was nervous. It was because I was *angry*.

"Get out of here, Allan," Elliot whispered loudly. "You don't know what you're talking about."

Allan didn't look at him. His squinty eyes, buried beneath his eyebrows, were focused squarely on me.

"Sawyer knows what I'm talking about. He's a monster. He doesn't belong in a school. I'm going to prove it, and when I do, they'll put him somewhere safe. Like in a zoo. Or some lab. Just as soon as they recognize him for the *freak* he is."

My hands were now shaking so hard that they were vibrating the table. I couldn't control myself anymore. I shot to my feet and screamed right in his face:

"Shut up, Allan! You don't know what you're talking about!"

At least, that's what it sounded like in my head.

Out loud, it sounded like:

ROOOOOOOOOOOAAAAAAARRRRRR!

It was the loudest sound I had ever heard in my life. And I couldn't just hear it. I could *feel* it. It shook the entire cafeteria. The tables rattled uncontrollably, and people grabbed for their lunches while also trying to cover their ears. It was kind of like we were all standing really close to a bass speaker, only about a hundred times louder.

I shut my mouth. The sound stopped.

There were about two seconds of silence. Absolute, perfect silence, as all three-hundred-something people in the cafeteria stared at me without moving a muscle.

Then the screaming started.

Every kid in the cafeteria jumped to his or her feet, knocked over their chair, and scrambled for the exit doors. Only Sylvie and Elliot stayed in their seats. Allan, who had been knocked on his butt by my roar, made two failed attempts to get to his feet before he finally crawled away as fast as he could. He was soon lost in the crowd that was fighting to fit through the double doors that led to the quad.

In less time than I would have thought possible, Sylvie, Elliot, and I were alone in the cafeteria.

I collapsed into my chair before my knees could give way. Across the table, Elliot looked sheet-white and shaken.

Only Sylvie looked unaffected. She passed us each a Pixy Stix and sat back in her chair with a contented smile on her face.

"*Finally*, some peace and quiet around here!"

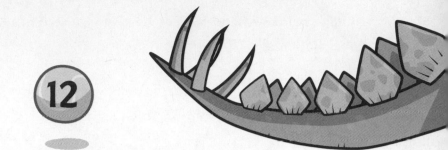

12

It Must've Been the Molé

I couldn't sit there one second longer. I just couldn't.

But I also didn't want to run into the crowd of students who had just vacated the cafeteria in terror. I had a feeling I wouldn't blend in.

So I went out the back way, the way that only teachers and cafeteria staff are allowed to go.

I left Sylvie and Elliot behind, walked through the deserted kitchen, and just kept opening doors until I found one that led outside. It opened up right next to the soccer field, which was blissfully empty of people.

I ran, holding my tail off the ground with one hand, until I was in the very center of the field. Then I stopped and stood still. I had no idea what I was doing there. I knew it wouldn't be long before someone would find me. Probably Animal Control. Or the police.

But for right now, this moment, I was in a big, empty, open space. Alone. With no one staring at me.

It felt…*nice*.

The weather was nice too. It was unseasonably warm for fall in Portland, and the sun was actually coming out from behind the clouds for once. I could feel its warm rays hitting my plates. I stretched my neck out and angled my back so that the sun would be able to reach as many of them as possible. I shivered in the warmth. It was the good kind of shiver, like stepping out into the sun after you've spent too long in air-conditioning.

There was a little bit of breeze too. I could feel it on my face. I was never really one to notice things like breezes, but this one caught my attention. I closed my eyes and felt the light wind pick up the very ends of my hair. I tried to use that to figure out which direction it was coming from. I didn't really know why I was doing that. It didn't make much sense to me. Until, slowly, as though I was obeying some long-forgotten instinct, I turned into the wind.

I felt an icy *woooooosh* as the breeze traveled over the top of my head and down my two rows of plates, spilling down my back like a waterfall of wind. I had always thought of my plates the way they were described in scientific journals, as "bony protrusions," but they were anything but that right then. They were *alive*. And as sensitive as fingertips as they drank in the sunshine and basked in the gentle touch of the wind.

I kind of wanted to squirm, the way Fanny did when I rubbed her belly in just the right spot. But I was afraid to move, afraid to lose the sensation. It was peaceful. For the very first time, my dinosaur parts didn't feel like bulky, awkward growths. In fact, they didn't even feel like *parts* anymore. They just felt like me.

It occurred to me that everybody, including me, had been talking about how I had "turned" part dinosaur over the summer. But that wasn't exactly true. Dinosaur had been in my DNA all along. I had always been part dinosaur; it had just taken me eleven years to grow the plates to prove it.

I could hear people in the distance. Shouting. At me. And at others to tell them they'd found me. They would be upon me soon. And even if they somehow missed me, standing out in the open, the dark clouds on the horizon would eventually roll in and take away the sunshine.

But until then, I would just stand here with my eyes closed. I didn't want this feeling to end. I just wanted to be happy. And I would be, for as long as they would let me. Happy to not hate that I was part dinosaur. For at least a minute or two more.

"I'm really sorry, Principal Mathis," I said, staring down at my hands. "I don't know what happened."

When I finally looked up, Principal Mathis was blinking at me from across her desk. Her hair looked bigger than usual today, which made her face look smaller. Which, in turn, made her look extremely mantis-like.

"What *happened* is that you lost your temper," she said. "What did Allan say to you?"

"Nothing," I mumbled, trying not to shiver. Seriously, why did the administration wing always have to be like twenty degrees colder than the rest of the school?

"At the beginning of this year, I told you to come straight to me if anyone started picking on you. I *know* Allan has been giving you a hard time, but I don't have anything to prove it. Why haven't you been to see me about him?"

I shrugged.

"Sawyer," she said, her voice taking a turn for the sharp. "*Why* won't you admit that Allan is bullying you? I can't help you if you don't tell me what happened."

"I don't—" I swallowed, somewhat painfully. My throat had been aching ever since the roar. "I don't want you to help me anymore."

"What?" Principal Mathis asked, sounding confused.

"Enough kids are already gone," I said, so quietly I could barely hear myself. I glanced up at her, worried that I had gone too far.

Principal Mathis wasn't looking at me. She was staring at the lone piece of artwork on her office wall, a framed quote that read:

He who opens a school door, closes a prison.

—*Victor Hugo*

"Not quite enough," she mumbled. Then she shook her head and turned back to me again.

"I want you to feel safe at this school, Sawyer."

"I do," I said quickly. "But what about them?"

"Them?" She blinked at me again.

"The kids who are gone," I persisted. I was pushing it, I knew that. But I *had* to find out.

Principal Mathis's face had no expression on it whatsoever.

"What about them?" she asked.

"Are they...safe?" I asked.

"Of course they're safe." Principal Mathis looked aghast. "What do you think has happened to them, Sawyer?"

I shrugged.

"I don't know. We just think—"

"*We?*" she demanded.

"*I,*" I corrected myself. There was no point in dragging Sylvie and Elliot into this. "*I* just wonder where they went. That's all."

Principal Mathis took a deep breath. After a moment or two more of staring at me, she opened her desk drawer and took out a brochure. She made as if to hand it to me, then hesitated.

"Can you keep a secret, Sawyer?"

"OK," I agreed.

She put the brochure in my hand.

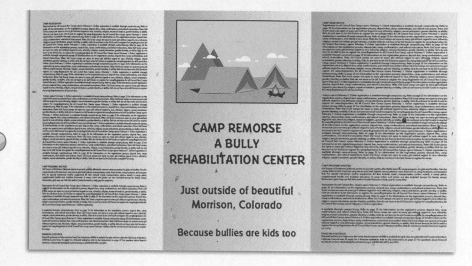

CAMP REMORSE
A BULLY
REHABILITATION CENTER

Just outside of beautiful
Morrison, Colorado

Because bullies are kids too

"I can see you are very concerned about your classmates, Sawyer," Principal Mathis said. "So I'll let you in on the secret. Because of the zero tolerance policy, all of the students who have bullied you since school began have been automatically expelled. But they have also been offered the opportunity to enroll in a six-week intensive program at Camp Remorse. Those who successfully complete the program will be welcomed back to school."

"Oh," I said. Was that it? Parker and the others weren't dead, they were just in Colorado? Suddenly, everything Elliot and Sylvie and I had speculated over the past few days seemed absurd. What had we been thinking? Of course ten kids hadn't just up and disappeared.

"Why is it a secret?" I asked Principal Mathis, as I skimmed through several of the program offerings inside the brochure, like "Hot Yoga for Hot Heads" and "The Art of Patience, Not Put-Downs."

She sat back in her chair and shrugged.

"Several of the parents are concerned about this incident damaging their child's future academic career. I have assured them that so long as their child graduates from the program, their expulsion will be reversed and removed from their permanent record. Assuming there are no future incidents, no one will ever have to know that their child attended Camp Remorse."

"Oh," I said again. That made sense.

Principal Mathis caught my eye over the edge of the program.

"They're not getting off without punishment, Sawyer," she said. Behind her glasses, her eyes were full of sincerity. "This is a tough program. It will make them think about what they did to you and how wrong it was. But it will also give them a chance to work through their problems and rejoin the school as better adjusted, more tolerant kids. I promise, not a single student will be allowed back into this school until they have demonstrated, to my satisfaction, that they have been fully rid of their need to bully."

I nodded vigorously, rather embarrassed by Principal Mathis's intense need to defend me.

But I was also kind of touched. I was pretty sure that our previous principal hadn't even known my name.

"I'll try not to roar again," I told her. "I didn't mean to. I think it might just be something that happens when I get angry. Or maybe when I eat spicy food. I'm not really sure. But I promise I won't bite anyone, like that kid in New Jersey."

"I've never thought you would bite anyone, Sawyer," Principal Mathis said. She stood, indicating that I should leave.

"But do try to keep the roaring under control. Two fifth graders who heard it had nervous breakdowns and had to be sent home for the day. Their parents were not pleased."

"Sorry," I muttered again, as I reached for the doorknob.

"Sawyer?"

"Yeah?" I turned back around.

Principal Mathis held out her hand.

"The brochure?"

"Oh, right…"

I handed her the brochure and left her office. Ms. Helen looked up as I did, then pressed a button on her fan that made it oscillate back and forth even faster than before.

I had to break my promise to Principal Mathis almost immediately, as Sylvie and Elliot were both waiting for me right outside the administration building. I felt sort of guilty about it, but I couldn't let the two of them go on thinking our classmates were dead or in trouble when I knew differently.

They didn't react how I'd imagined.

"Camp *what*?" Elliot scoffed.

"That sounds made up," Sylvie seconded.

"I saw a brochure!" I insisted. "There were classes, and a logo, and it's just outside of Colorado, and—"

"Totally made up," Sylvie concluded with a sniff.

"Well," Elliot hedged. "I guess it does sort of explain why Parker's mom said she missed him."

Sylvie shook her head.

"You guys are so gullible. Camp *Remorse*? That's just ridiculous. Principal Mathis is a total liar."

"No, she's *not!*" I fired back. "She's trying to help me. You don't know anything, Sylvie."

"Oh, I know stuff!" Sylvie snipped, putting her hands on her hips and glaring at me from under her hoodie. "And even if I didn't, I know better than to be a trusting nitwit who just—"

"Shhh!" Elliot broke in frantically. "It's her!"

Sylvie's jaw snapped shut as Principal Mathis came striding through the administration building doors.

Even in her enormous heels, which made a sharp *click–click* on the ground as she passed us, the principal was still only a bit taller than Sylvie and me. Which meant that she was about a foot shorter than Elliot.

"Hello, Principal Mathis," Elliot said, smiling and giving her a goofy wave.

"Hello there," Principal Mathis said, smiling up at him as she breezed by. She seemed to be in a hurry. She barely nodded at Sylvie and me as she *click-clicked* down toward the parking lot and took a sharp left.

Sylvie watched with narrowed eyes as Principal Mathis disappeared around the side of the science wing.

"I'm following her," she declared, then looked warningly at Elliot and me. "You coming?"

I hesitated. So did Elliot.

"What if we don't?" Elliot inquired.

Sylvie shrugged.

"Then don't blame me if you both end up at *Camp Remorse*."

13

The Obstacle Course

As soon as Elliot and I moved to follow Sylvie down the steps of the administration building, it started to rain. Hard.

Which was actually pretty helpful. Turns out it's easy to follow people in the rain. Especially when they pull an enormous yellow umbrella out of their purse and hold it up like a beacon over their head. Which is exactly what Principal Mathis did. Sylvie, Elliot, and I just had to stay close enough to keep the yellow umbrella in sight. Plus, the rain was so loud we didn't even have to be that quiet.

I found myself hoping that Principal Mathis was leading us to the library or to the girls' restroom. Or somewhere else so boring that Sylvie would lose interest in her and stop forcing me and Elliot to accompany her on her stealth missions.

But then I realized that we were going in the opposite direction from the library. And then we passed three girls' restrooms without stopping. By the time we went by the art wing and entered an area at the very back of the school where the portable classrooms were kept, even I had to admit something weird was going on.

Elliot and I had both had an art class in one of the portable class-rooms last year while the roof on the art wing was being fixed. But as far as I knew, the portables were empty this year.

Sylvie motioned for us to slow down and hide behind a row of bushes, just as the principal reached the door of the farthest portable. Principal Mathis closed her umbrella and leaned it carefully against the wall beside the door. She was holding a key chain in her hand. There was a single key dangling from a red circular disk the size of a silver dollar.

Then Principal Mathis suddenly whirled around.

I froze; so did Elliot and Sylvie. The rain ran off the hood of my jacket and dripped from the tip of my nose. I held my breath.

The bush was not thick. I could see Principal Mathis perfectly through a cantaloupe-sized hole in the foliage. We were *so* about to be caught.

"This is stupid," Elliot muttered, crouched down awkwardly beside me so that his knees were practically in his face. "She can *totally* see us."

"Wait," Sylvie commanded him. "Just wait."

We did.

Principal Mathis began a left-to-right scan of the area behind her. It was hard to tell, because I was too far away to see her eyes behind her thick glasses, but I was 90 percent sure that her eyes swept right over our bush. But they didn't stop, not until they got all the way to the edge of her vision on the right.

Then she nodded, put the key in the lock, and let herself into the portable.

◊◊◊

"Interesting," Sylvie marveled.

"She didn't see us?" Elliot asked, incredulous, as he wiped the rain from his face. A losing fight, considering it was raining harder than ever. "How did she not see us?"

"Maybe it was the rain?" I guessed.

But I knew that wasn't it. I didn't know what *it* was, but there was definitely something strange happening here.

"Sylvie, what's going on?" I asked. Because of the three of us, she seemed the most likely to know.

"Let's go see what's in the portable," Sylvie suggested, and motioned for us to follow her around the back of the building.

There were two large windows there, covered with heavy blinds. But the slats were large enough that we could see through them if we squinted.

All the desks inside the portable had been pushed to one side, leaving a wide, open space in the center. The space was filled with obstacles: a balance beam, an inflatable tunnel, a wooden wall that came up to about head height, a climbing rope attached to the ceiling, and pull-up bars. A trail of tires continued into the portable next door. The wall between the two rooms had been removed, so there was now twice the normal amount of space inside.

Which was good, because there were at least ten kids running the obstacle course in a clockwise circle.

The whole setup looked like the sort of thing a desperate gym teacher would construct on a rainy day. But there was something off about the scene. I was trying to figure out what it was when one of the kids suddenly fell off the balance beam.

He hit the ground, then rolled right toward our window and out of sight. After a moment, the kid popped up again about a foot away from my face.

I froze as a pair of green eyes looked right at me through a mop of red hair and a mess of freckles.

Brad blinked and gave me a slightly unfocused smile. Then he lurched to his feet, staggered back toward the balance beam, and scrambled back up.

No one else came that close to my window, but now that I knew what to look for, I saw it all: Mary's long, black ponytail swinging back and forth as she jumped from tire to tire; Jeremy hitching up his overalls as he used a rope to pull himself over the wall; the pink sparkles on Emma's shoes flashing as she wove in and out of a line of poles.

"Holy cow," Elliot marveled beside me.

The kids who had been kicked out of school were, most definitely, not at Camp Remorse.

Sylvie was right. Principal Mathis was a big, fat liar.

We could see her inside the portable too. She made a quick survey of the room, patted Mary on the head, and then went back out the front door.

The three of us peeked around the side of the portable and watched as she hurried back toward the administration building under the cover of her yellow umbrella. She was twirling the red key chain around with one hand, and she didn't look back once.

Elliot appeared to be having difficulty breathing.

"This is…" He trailed off, and looked around helplessly. "This is…*crazy*. First, they were missing. Then, they were at a bully rehab camp. Now they're in a building at the back of the school?"

"I told you," Sylvie said, leading us back around to the front. "Principal Mathis lied to you."

She walked right up to the front of the portable and pounded on the door. We waited expectantly, but no one answered.

Sylvie reached for the doorknob, gave a yelp, and pulled her hand back. I could have sworn I saw a spark fly from the tip of her finger.

"Ow!" she complained, sucking on her hand. "The doorknob is electrified!"

"Let's try the window," I suggested.

I went around back again and knocked hard on the window. I squinted through the blinds, but all I could see was an endless circle of kids, their faces tight with grim determination, somehow managing to keep their distance from one another as they tackled one obstacle after another.

"Hey!" I shouted. "Mary! Emma! Can you hear me?"

There was no response. They just kept running, climbing, and balancing, as though the obstacle course was the only thing in the world. They all had the same glazed look as Brad. Something was very, very wrong here.

These didn't look like the kind of windows you could open from the outside, but I reached out to touch the metal frame anyway, just in case.

I jumped when the electrical charge shot into my fingers and up my arm.

"Ow!" I yelled.

"Would you guys stop touching things?" Elliot exclaimed, his eyes large. "We have to call the police!" He plunged his hand into his pocket and dug around for his phone.

Sylvie grabbed his arm and shook her head firmly. "No, Elliot. You can't do that."

"Are you joking?" I demanded, and pointed to the window. "There are *kids* in there! You were right, OK? Principal Mathis *is* a liar. And we have to tell someone! Before something happens to them!"

Sylvie shook her head again. "No. You guys don't understand. This isn't something the police can help with."

"What do you mean?" I looked at her suspiciously. "What aren't you telling us, Sylvie? How did you know Principal Mathis was lying? How do you know these things?"

"I just know, OK?"

"Not good enough!" I yelled. I could hear hysteria enter my voice, but I didn't care. Given the situation, I thought hysteria was rather appropriate. It was Sylvie's cool-as-a-cucumber calmness that seemed wrong to me.

"Sawyer, calm down," she advised me.

"No!" I yelled. "I won't! Not until you explain things. It was your idea to be suspicious of Principal Mathis. And you were right. How did you know she was lying to us?"

"Because…" she answered, still dead calm and searching for the right words. "Because I don't think Principal Mathis is what she appears to be."

"What does *that* mean?" I demanded. "You just got to this school. Did you know Principal Mathis before, from somewhere else?"

"No."

"Then how do you know anything about her?"

"I just know."

I shook my head.

"*How* do you know?"

Sylvie bit her lip. She looked caught. *I* had caught her.

"I know…" Sylvie began. She looked around nervously, but there was just the three of us standing there. Us, and a whole lot of rain.

"I know because of *this*."

Sylvie yanked off the hood of her sweatshirt. Her hair was immediately soaked. The poofy curls were beaten down flat, making her look a couple of inches shorter than usual.

She reached up both hands and started rooting around under the hair at the crown of her head. All the while, Sylvie's eyes bounced intensely from my face, to Elliot's, and back to mine again.

There were two loud *snaps* as she unclipped her silver barrettes. As soon as she untangled them from her soggy curls, two pale pink antennae sprang free and stood up straight, right on the top of her head.

And that was how Elliot and I found out that Sylvie was a Martian.

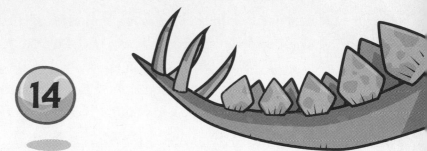

Martians, Martians, Everywhere...

"A half-Martian, actually," Sylvie corrected me after school that same day.

We were at her mother's restaurant again. Mama Juarez's Cucina was open to the public now and, from the looks of things, it was becoming popular very quickly. It wasn't even dinnertime yet, and already almost every table was full.

In spite of the crowd, the three of us were given a prime booth. Those are the perks of being friends with the owner's daughter. That and free chips, which Elliot and Sylvie ate while I demolished a large bowl of greens (minus the molé this time, just in case). Our adventure in the rain had given us healthy appetites.

"So let me get this straight," Elliot said. "Your mom"—he looked toward the kitchen door, behind which Mrs. Juarez had just disappeared—"she's human?"

"Yup. And my dad's a Martian."

I looked warily at the people sitting around us. Sylvie was wearing her hood up, and underneath, I knew her antennae were fastened down with clips again. Now that I knew to look closely, I guess her skin was a little bit smoother and shinier than normal human skin. And her eyes may have been a little bit rounder. But other than that, she looked like an ordinary girl.

She was also making no effort to keep her voice down at all. If anyone around us was paying attention...

But the people around us were all busy enjoying their food. I don't think anybody even noticed my plates or my tail, let alone that there was a Martian at our table.

Elliot was still trying to get all of the details straight.

"So if your mom's human and your dad's a...a M-Martian," he ventured. I could tell that he couldn't quite believe he was saying that last word out loud. "How did they meet?"

"Match.com," Sylvie answered, totally straight-faced.

Elliot's eyes bulged.

"Seriously?"

"No." Sylvie giggled and stuffed another chip into her mouth. "My dad is a restaurateur."

"A what?" I asked.

"A restaurateur. It means he owns a bunch of restaurants. He specializes in exotic cuisine. He met my mom while they were both in culinary school in Artesia, just south of Roswell, New Mexico. When they graduated, they got married, moved to Mars, and opened a chain of Tex-Mex-Martian fusions places. They're *really* popular in Mars."

"You mean, 'on' Mars, don't you?" Elliot asked.

Sylvie shook her head. She was smiling. More than I had ever seen her smile since I'd met her. Maybe she hadn't really liked having to keep her Martianness a secret. She seemed very relieved to finally be able to talk about it with us.

"No, I mean 'in Mars,'" she was saying to Elliot. "Martians live underground. So it's more accurate to say that we live 'in' Mars, as opposed to 'on.'"

Elliot looked at me across the table.

"My head hurts," he announced, and lowered his forehead onto his crossed arms.

Sylvie gave him a slightly concerned look, then reached for another chip.

"You said your dad was away on a business trip," I remembered suddenly. "You said that he lived 'a little bit outside of Portland.'"

"That wasn't *exactly* a lie," Sylvie said, delicately nibbling a chip. "Mars *is* outside of Portland. And it's a lot closer to Portland than, say, Neptune or Saturn. So relatively speaking, Mars *is* just a little bit outside of Portland."

Elliot groaned into his arms.

"And your dad is on—er, *in*—Mars now?" I persisted.

Sylvie nodded.

"Until he comes here to get me, yeah, he is. He's working. When my parents separated last year, my mom brought me back to Earth. To New Mexico. But it was a little bit too sunny there for me." She fingered her nose, which now had no trace of the sunburn she had had on the day we met her. "Martian skin is really sensitive. I think it's because of the whole living underground thing. So we moved here."

"Because there's not as much sun?" I guessed.

"Yeah. That, and my mom had a contact in the Portland culinary world. That's how she got this restaurant up and running." She gestured around us. "It's the first one she's done without my dad. It's kind of a big deal to her."

"Oh," I said, pausing to think through everything Sylvie had just disclosed. I was pretty sure Elliot was doing the same thing, only he was doing it with his face down on the table. "So…you said that all of this has something to do with Principal Mathis?"

"Oh, yeah." Sylvie sat up a little bit straighter. "I'm pretty sure she's a Martian too."

"Of course she is," Elliot mumbled into his arms.

Sylvie shot him another concerned look.

"Is he going to be OK?" she asked me.

"He's processing," I told her. "Just give him a minute."

"OK."

We chewed in silence for several minutes before Elliot finally raised his head out of his arms.

"So," he said, "you're a Martian."

"Half-Martian," said Sylvie. "We've covered that."

"And our principal is a Martian too?" Elliot continued.

"I didn't say that," Sylvie corrected him. "I said I was 'pretty sure' she's a Martian."

"What do you mean by that?" I asked.

"Well." Sylvie considered this for a moment. "It's just a guess. But I'm more sure now than I was when I first got to this school."

"What made you more sure?" I asked.

"Well, she's pretty short. And Martians are pretty short. I've never seen her antennae, but she styles her hair pretty big, so she could be hiding them under there. That's two things," Sylvie mused, ticking them off on her fingers as she went. "Oh, and she wears really thick glasses. That's a big giveaway."

"Glasses?" I asked. "Martians wear glasses?"

Sylvie took a sip of her Coke and nodded.

"Most of us, yeah. Our eyesight sucks. At least, it does when we're aboveground."

I thought back to earlier that day, when Principal Mathis had looked right at our totally obvious hiding spot without seeing us.

"The only people who have worse eyesight than Martians are the Jupiterians," Sylvie was saying. "I think it's because they come from such a gaseous planet. Their eyesight evolved differently than everyone else's."

"Jupiter!" Elliot exclaimed. "There are people on Jupiter too?"

"There are people on almost every planet, Elliot," Sylvie retorted, digging a handful of Pixy Stix out of her sweatshirt pocket. She set half of them on the table in front of her and tore the tops off the other half with one, large *riiiiip*. "You just have to know where to look."

"But *you* don't wear glasses," I pointed out.

Sylvie leaned toward me and pointed to her eye. I looked closely at the light brown circle around her pupil, and I could just make out the faint curve of a lens.

"Contacts," she explained, then she leaned her head back and emptied all of the open Pixy Stix into her mouth. "But I barely need them. I had the best eyesight in my entire school back home."

She lowered her chin and batted her eyelashes proudly. "I have my mom's eyes."

"So what you're saying," I said, "is that we should suspect that all short, big-haired, glasses-wearing people are Martians?"

Sylvie shrugged.

"Probably not *all* of them are Martians," she allowed. "But a fair amount of them probably are. There are more Martians on Earth than you might think."

"And our principal is one of them," Elliot surmised.

"Probably."

"And she's keeping ten of the kids in our class locked in a secret classroom in the back of our school?" Elliot continued.

"Yes," Sylvie agreed, looking pleased that Elliot had finally caught up.

"And *why* is she keeping them locked up?" I asked.

Sylvie shrugged.

"I don't know."

Elliot's eyes suddenly grew huge.

"Martians don't…you know…*eat* humans, do they?"

"No!" Sylvie exclaimed, looking disgusted. "Why would they do that?"

"I don't know," Elliot said, looking vaguely embarrassed and muttering something about *The Twilight Zone* that I didn't quite catch. He motioned to the Pixy Stix. "What about the candy? Is that a Martian thing too?"

Sylvie shrugged.

"Actually, it's more of an Earth thing. Earth candy is full of high-fructose corn syrup and processed sugar."

"So…" Elliot prompted her.

"That stuff is illegal on pretty much every other planet," Sylvie informed him.

"So there's no candy on Mars?" I asked.

"There's candy," Sylvie said, making a face as she ripped open the remaining Pixy Stix. "But we don't have anything like *this*."

She tipped her head back and poured so much sugar into her mouth that a small cloud of dust gathered around her face. When she looked at us again, there was a sprinkling of pink powder on her nose. And a giant smile on her face.

"Well," I said, trying to get back to the point. "The kids in the portable are not made out of sugar. So if Principal Mathis is not eating them, what *is* she doing with them?"

"I don't know," Sylvie said, licking her lips. "But we're going to find out. It's time to go back to our original plan."

"Our original plan." Elliot scrunched his nose as he tried to think. "Which was…"

"We're going to break into Principal Mathis's office," Sylvie reminded him. "*Tonight*."

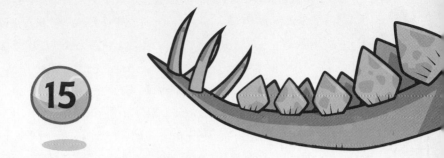

15

Breaking In

Later that night, when I tiptoed out of my room and down to the front door, I was not surprised when sixteen pounds of fluffy, white rage came barreling down the stairs after me.

We didn't have an alarm system in our house. Fanny, who slept at the foot of my parents' bed with one eye open, her tiny paws itching to defend her home, was more than adequate for that purpose. But I was ready for her.

"Fanny!" I whispered, standing my ground at the foot of the stairs and holding a spare tennis ball right in her line of vision.

She skidded to a halt.

I threw the ball down the hall, toward the kitchen. When she tore after it, I quietly slipped out the front door. Then I waited, safely hidden in the darkness of the porch, and listened hard for a full minute. Nothing. No sound anywhere. My suburban Portland neighborhood was fast asleep.

I shook my head as I walked down our driveway. It had been *shockingly* easy to escape my house, with my parents being none the wiser. I filed this information away for later use during my teenage years.

My school is only six blocks from my house, and I made it there in record time. I felt very exposed, walking on the quiet streets alone. The streetlights felt like spotlights, and I was kind of freaked out by the sight of my own shadow. From the side, all you could see were my plates and the long curve of my tail. There was nothing human-looking about my shadowy silhouette at all.

I was glad to finally leave the streetlights behind and duck into the relative darkness in front of the administration building.

Elliot was already there. He was wearing a black ski cap, a black sweatshirt, and black sweatpants. In one hand, he held a flashlight, which was switched off. He looked like the dictionary definition of "burglar."

I was wearing my blue raincoat, modified to accommodate my plates, over plaid pajama bottoms and sneakers. It hadn't occurred to me that our midnight heist would require a change of clothes.

"Where's Sylvie?" I asked him.

"Not here yet," he answered, shifting his flashlight nervously from hand to hand. "Do you think she's even coming?"

"This was her idea," I reminded him.

"Yeah…I was thinking about that on the way here."

"Oh?" I encouraged him.

"How do we know she's not on Principal Mathis's side? I mean, they're both Martians, right? Maybe they're setting us up."

"For what?" I asked, peering into the surrounding darkness.

I didn't think for one minute that Sylvie was in cahoots with Principal Mathis.

"Remember that *Twilight Zone* episode when aliens come to Earth?" he asked.

"Are you sure that only happened in *one* episode?" I asked finally, taking a mental inventory of all of the *Twilight Zones* Elliot had made me watch over the years.

"You know the one I'm talking about," Elliot insisted. "The one where they say they're here to help humans and they have this giant book about how they are going to 'serve man'?"

"I guess…"

"It turned out to be a cookbook, Sawyer. That's all I'm saying."

"Elliot," came a voice from the darkness behind him. "I already told you that Martians don't eat Earthlings."

Elliot gasped dramatically and whirled around as Sylvie materialized out of the night and walked up the steps to meet us. As usual, she was wearing her orange sweatshirt, hood up. Strangely, she still looked less conspicuous than Elliot.

Elliot eyed her suspiciously.

"Isn't that exactly what you would say if you *were* planning to eat us?" he asked.

Sylvie opened her mouth to respond, but I cut her off.

"Why don't we concentrate on figuring out how we're going to get inside the school?" I suggested.

Sylvie motioned to the door.

"It should be unlocked."

It was my turn to eye her suspiciously; she shrugged.

"Try it," she suggested.

I reached for the door. Despite Sylvie's confident tone, I was very surprised when it opened easily.

"How did you do that?" Elliot demanded of Sylvie. "This place is usually locked down like a prison."

Sylvie wiggled her eyebrows at him.

"A Martian never reveals her sources," she said mysteriously.

"No, that's reporters," Elliot said. "*Reporters* never reveal their sources."

"Oh," said Sylvie, looking momentarily deflated. Then she brightened. "Well, it's the same thing for Martians."

She reached past me to open the door wider. I turned, intending to tell Elliot to lay off Sylvie, but I was blinded by headlights before I could get a word out.

"Car!" Elliot hissed. "*Hide!*"

Sylvie let go of the door and dove behind a pillar on the right side of the building. Elliot and I ran to hide behind the pillar on the left side.

The door swung shut with an agonizingly loud *click*, and then there was silence.

The car had the words "Viking Security" printed on the door, and a blue siren was stuck on top of the roof. The siren was off, which I thought was a good sign, but the car was doing a slow circle of the parking lot directly in front of the administration building.

I tucked myself as far back into the shelter of the pillar as I could go, being careful not to squish Elliot with my tail, while the probable events of the next day flashed before my eyes.

The police. Our parents being called. The grounding.

The headline: "Dinosaur Hybrid Caught Breaking into School."

Thanks to the T. rex in Jersey, everybody already thought dinosaur hybrids were violent. Now, thanks to me, they'd also think we have criminal tendencies. Great.

The car's headlights swept over the administration building door three times. Each time, I held my breath and waited for the sound of the engine turning off and a door opening. But it never came. After the third time, I heard Sylvie's loud whisper.

"We're OK! The car's leaving!"

I looked around the pillar again, just as the car disappeared around the corner, toward the faculty parking lot.

The three of us all let out giant, relieved breaths and ran to get inside before the security guard came back.

Once the door had closed behind us, Elliot held up his flashlight, but I shook my head. It was even darker inside the school than it had been outside, but we couldn't risk a light. The security guard might see it. Even from a distance. We used our hands to help us creep by the front desk.

I breathed a sigh of relief when I felt my way past Ms. Helen's empty desk. I had half expected to find her sitting there in her usual spot, glowering at us in the dark from behind her fan and her woefully out-of-date solar system model.

It did occur to me that we had just proven, definitively, that Ms. Helen was not, in fact, permanently attached to her desk. Too bad we wouldn't be able to tell anybody.

It was easier to see once we got inside Principal Mathis's office.

Her front window overlooked a large streetlight, which filled the room with a dim, but welcome glow.

"What exactly are we looking for?" Elliot asked, looking around hesitantly.

"Anything out of the ordinary," Sylvie answered, heading straight for Principal Mathis's desk. "I'll check her laptop. You guys look everywhere else."

Principal Mathis didn't have much stuff in her office. So *everywhere else* was just a large, wooden cabinet on the back wall. Elliot and I walked up to examine it.

It was a huge, antiquey-looking wood armoire with metal details. The two big doors on the front had fancy handles in the shape of grinning lizards.

"I don't think it's locked," Elliot said quietly, running his hand over one of the lizards and jiggling it slightly. "I think if I just pull on it—"

"Careful," I admonished him. "Don't break anything."

"It's too heavy to break," he informed me, tugging hard but not budging the door one bit. He stepped back for a moment, then wrapped both hands around the left lizard head for a second attempt.

The door still did not move.

"Here." I stepped up next to him and grabbed the right lizard, bracing my foot against the side of the armoire for leverage. "On three. One, two—"

"Three!" Elliot grunted, and we yanked in unison.

The doors both swung open, and Elliot tumbled backward. I swayed back as well, but managed to stay upright with a little help from my tail.

That's why I was the one who saw Principal Mathis's head staring at me, eyeless, from the shelf inside the armoire.

16

Red Vines and Victor Hugo

I'm only slightly ashamed to admit that I screamed like a little girl. I like to think there may have been the tiniest of dinosaur-worthy roars in there as well, maybe near the tail end of my ear-splitting shriek. But I don't think there was. It all sounded pretty high-pitched to me. Nothing like when I had lost my temper in the cafeteria.

"What? What is it?" Elliot scrambled to his feet. I slammed the door of the armoire before he could see what was inside.

"Shhhhhhhh!" Sylvie hissed at us. She was sitting at Principal Mathis's desk, and her irritated scowl was lit up by the computer screen in front of her. She made no move to join us in front of the armoire of death. "*Quiet!* What did you find?"

"P-P-P-Principal M-M-M-Mathis." I pointed feebly at the lizard head door. "Her—her *head*."

"Ew!" Elliot declared, and immediately opened the door to see for himself. I stepped out of the way so I wouldn't have to see it again.

"It's probably just her mask," Sylvie said, sounding bored as she continued to stare at the computer screen and punch keys. "Her *human* mask. She's a full Martian, remember? She needs a disguise to fit in here."

"*Awesome.*" Elliot appeared around the side of the armoire, holding Principal Mathis's face in one hand. Inside the armoire, I spotted a blank mannequin head. The stretchy plastic face must have been draped over it, causing the illusion of Principal Mathis's severed head.

I watched Elliot stretch the face out in his hands, crumple it into a handful of skin, then stretch it out again. A horrible thought occurred to me.

"Sylvie," I said, looking hard at her face through the glow of the computer. "You're not wearing a human mask, are you?"

She laughed.

"No. I don't need a mask. I'm half human, remember? And I take after my mother."

"Good," I said, and shuddered.

"I've got to get something like this for Halloween," Elliot said, mostly to himself as he kept playing with the mask.

Still disgusted by the whole thing, I turned away from Elliot and opened the armoire door to see what else was inside.

The topmost shelf held the now-naked mannequin head. There was also a metal stand full of business cards and several rows of white boxes.

There wasn't enough light to read the tiny print on the business cards, so I stuffed one in my pocket for later and grabbed one of the white boxes instead.

Inside, there was a tangle of pink straps and buckles. I had to turn the whole thing over several times in my hands before I realized that it was a harness. It looked kind of like the one that my mom had bought for Fanny, only Principal Mathis's was bigger and bright pink. It was also covered with cheap-looking plastic gemstones.

Next to the harness was a spray can. I held up the can to catch the light from outside, and I could just barely make out the words "GOOD BOY" written in large, white letters. Underneath, in slightly smaller letters, were the words "BEHAVIOR MODIFICATION SPRAY."

Principal Mathis must have a dog. A big dog, based on the size of the harness.

The bottom shelf was crammed full of boxes. They had been arranged kind of like a Jenga puzzle, so that every single inch of space on the shelf was taken up. I wiggled a box free.

Red Vines.

The entire shelf was stuffed full of Red Vines.

Weird. Just weird.

"Hey, Sawyer!"

Elliot peered around the side of the cabinet. He was wearing Principal Mathis's face over his own.

"Detention!" he declared, through Principal Mathis's lips, shaking an accusatory finger at me. "We have a zero tolerance policy here, Mr. Bronson!"

"*Boys,*" Sylvie scolded us. "I need a hand over here."

I smacked Elliot on the side of his head and went to join Sylvie in front of the computer.

"There's nothing strange on her hard drive," she informed us. "Just school stuff. The school probably owns the computer, so she wouldn't risk putting anything on there that might give her away as a Martian."

"Then what are we still looking at the computer for?" Elliot asked, wearing his own face again and squinting at the bright screen from the other side of Sylvie.

"I want to get into her personal email. I think I know her username, but I don't know her password."

Sylvie typed a few keys and hit ENTER.

Access denied. Password does not match username.

Sylvie bit her lip in frustration.

"Can't you hack it?" Elliot asked.

Sylvie turned to him, an accusatory expression on her face.

"What, just because I'm half Martian, you think I'm a computer nerd?

Elliot shrugged.

"I don't know. You've got to be more advanced than us, right? I mean, you got to Earth somehow. And no humans have walked on Mars yet."

"Martian *scientists* may be more advanced," Sylvie said, "but I'm eleven. I only assigned myself the computer because I'm pretty sure I'm better at it than you. But that's not really saying much, is it? If you—"

"Guys," I interrupted. "This isn't helping. We need to think. If you were Principal Mathis, what would your password be?"

"Mantis?" Elliot suggested, looking only half serious.

"I already tried every variation of her name I could think of," Sylvie said.

"What about her birthday?" I suggested.

"I don't know her birthday," Sylvie said, with a shrug. "People choose passwords that are meaningful to them in some way. But she doesn't have much personal stuff around. It's hard to guess what would mean something to her." She gestured at the principal's desk, which was completely bare except for the computer, her nameplate, and a small stack of manila folders.

"Try 'Red Vines,'" I suggested, thinking of the cabinet.

Access denied.

"'Licorice,'" I tried again.

Access denied.

"This is making me hungry," Elliot complained, eyeing the bottom shelf of the cabinet. "Do you think Mathis would miss one box of Red Vines?"

"Yes," Sylvie answered immediately.

"Really?" Elliot looked disappointed. "How much candy can one Martian eat?"

"She's probably selling it," Sylvie explained. "There's a huge black market for Earth candy on Mars. All those Red Vines would be worth a *fortune* there."

I turned my attention back to our password problem. Suddenly, I remembered the harness.

"I think she has a dog," I ventured. "Dog? Puppy? Canine?"

Access denied. Access denied. Access denied.

"This is going to take all night," Elliot complained, looking at his watch and yawning. "My dad gets up for work at four thirty. I have to sneak back into my house before then."

Out of ideas, I looked around the office for help. Principal Mathis's lone piece of artwork caught my eye:

He who opens a school door, closes a prison.

—Victor Hugo

"Try 'Hugo,'" I suggested.

Sylvie typed the four letters, and suddenly Principal Mathis's inbox appeared on screen.

"Nice," Elliot said, and leaned over Sylvie's shoulder.

I frowned.

"Martians use Gmail?" I asked skeptically.

Sylvie nodded, her face serious. "Google started on Mars, you know. Earth is just their beta-testing ground."

She scrolled through screen after screen of mundane emails, mostly to and from teachers and other school personnel.

"Boring," Elliot declared. "Principal Mathis is the most uninteresting alien *ever.*"

"Wait," Sylvie said. "This might be something."

She clicked on an email from someone named "Client J."

From: clientj@jupiterpet.com
To: MMathis@jackjames.com

Dear Mathilda,

Attached please find my completed purchase order for the shipment we discussed. My buyers are very eager to acquire their new pets and are also interested in seeing your line of accessories. I trust you will provide feeding instructions, as well as assurances that all specimens are purebred. Several of my clients have small children and are concerned about the potentially aggressive nature of hybrids. Please see the purchase order for more detailed specifications on this matter.

Sincerely,
J.P. Tabar
Executive VP, Jupiter's Finest Pet Emporium

Our mission: to find you a pet as unique as you are!

"Pets?" Elliot read aloud, from behind me. "Principal Mathis sells pets?"

Thinking of something, I pulled the business card out of my pocket and held it up so I could read it by the light of the computer screen.

Mathilda C. Mathis
Senior Vice President

Exotic Exports

Purveyor of Rare Pets and Sweet Treats
Offices on Mars, Jupiter, and (Coming Soon!) Venus

"I guess so," I said, although something about this whole thing wasn't making much sense to me. Why would Principal Mathis be hiding a classroom full of students if her secret job was selling pets?

There was a faint squeal of car brakes outside. Elliot, who was closest to the window, ran over and peeked through the open blinds.

"The security guard is back!"

"The computer!" I yelled, slamming the laptop shut. "He'll be able to see the light!"

"Wait!" Sophie grabbed the computer, knelt under the desk, and opened it again. "I want to see the attachment to this email—I'm downloading it now."

"He's getting out of the car!" Elliot exclaimed from the window.

"Sylvie!" I exclaimed, looking nervously toward the window. "We don't have time to read that! We've got to go!"

"I'm printing it!" Sylvie announced, still under the desk. "Where's the printer?"

I spotted it over on top of the bookshelf. I fumbled around in the dark for the power button, basically just pushing buttons until something flashed green.

"He's coming up the steps!" Elliot squealed, backing away from the window. "We've got to get out of here!"

"Get the email, Sawyer!" Sylvie ordered, running for the door of the office. Elliot followed her.

I felt around the paper tray on the front of the printer, but it was empty.

"It's not here!" I whispered. "It didn't print!"

"Forget about it! Let's *go*!" Elliot implored.

I followed them into the front office. Elliot scooted past Ms. Helen's desk and headed for the back door. Besides the front door, where the security guard was, it was the only way out of the building.

It was a good plan, except that the back door was at the end of a long hallway, immediately opposite the front door. There was no way we would make it, not without being seen.

I grabbed the back of Elliot's shirt and pulled him back into the front office just as the door swung open.

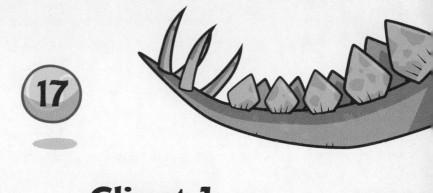

Client J

Sylvie dove under Ms. Helen's desk while Elliot and I both wedged ourselves underneath the large counter that separated the main office from the rest of the administration building. My tail, pulled tight against us like a seat belt, was the only thing keeping us from bursting out of the cramped space. Elliot's elbow was jammed into my side, and his fingernails were digging into the end of my tail. But I was trying too hard not to breathe to care about any of that.

I couldn't see the security guard, but I could hear his footsteps on the linoleum floor, and I could see his flashlight making wide arcs around the office. It lit up the front desk, the file cabinets, and the piles of paper waiting to be organized. It swung to the left; soon, it would illuminate Ms. Helen's desk, with its model solar system, the printer—

The printer.

There was a small printer on Ms. Helen's desk, right next to the fan. Approximately three inches from the top of Sylvie's hoodie, a green, flashing light was announcing that a print job had been completed. And the evidence was right there, waiting to be collected in the paper tray.

Why hadn't we run when we had the chance?

Even if we did get away, which wasn't looking very likely, the email proved that somebody had been in Principal Mathis's office that night. She would know that somebody was on to her.

The footsteps stopped abruptly, and the flashlight beam stopped, inches before hitting Ms. Helen's desk.

The footsteps started again, and a door creaked open. From my vantage point underneath the counter, I could see the security guard let himself into Principal Mathis's office.

I looked back toward the desk just as a tiny hand floated up from underneath. In one smooth move, Sylvie's nimble fingers hit the power button and the green light vanished. There was a slight rustling sound as she snatched the incriminating printout from the paper tray and brought it down, into the relative safety underneath the desk.

Not one second later, the security guard emerged from the principal's office. He closed the door behind him, turned his flashlight off, and walked back toward the front door of the building.

"Seeing things," he mumbled to himself, as he let himself out and locked the door behind him. A short time later, we heard the sound of a car engine slowly fade into the distance.

Elliot unclenched his fingers from my tail and tumbled out from underneath the desk.

"Close one!" he exclaimed. Elliot's face lit up with excitement—I'm not sure he'd had this much fun in years.

I crawled out after him, wincing as all of my squashed plates sprung back into place. Sylvie was already out from under Ms. Helen's desk, holding the piece of paper up so it caught the dim light from a nearby window.

"I don't get it," Elliot said. "Mathis sells pets? That's her big secret?"

"Uh-oh," said Sylvie, her eyes locked on the printout.

"What?" I asked, coming over so that I could read it too. "What does it say? What kind of pets does Mathis sell?"

Sylvie looked up at me, her eyes like shiny quarters in the faint light.

"Kids," she said. "Principal Mathis sells kids. That's why she's keeping Parker and the others. She's going to sell them. As *pets*."

18

The Runaround

We've got to go to the police," Elliot concluded the following morning.

"Slow down, please," I pleaded, panting.

Coach Carpenter, having apparently run out of ways to torture us *indoors*, was forcing us to do laps around the school. For the entire period. No exceptions for those of us with heavy dinosaur parts that jiggled uncomfortably at even the slowest jog.

Or for those of us who are extra sensitive to the sun. Sylvie lumbered along beside me, wearing her usual sweatshirt over her gym uniform and sweating heavily. Her face was already bright red. The extra sunscreen she had smeared all over her face had all dripped off somewhere around the second lap.

I had the printout from last night in my pocket. I had it memorized by now, but I still took it out every once in a while, just to make sure it really said what I remembered:

PURCHASE ORDER

Description of Goods: Thirteen human juveniles.

Specifications: In good health, a variety of colors, and gentle temperaments suitable for close contact with children. Purebreds only. No hybrids will be accepted. Attempted delivery of a hybrid will void this contract and jeopardize future business relations between the two parties.

Delivery: Delivery will be made when all thirteen juveniles have been secured.

The agreement went on to discuss pricing, customs issues, insurance, and something called "indemnification in the event of casualty or loss," but all I could think about were the jeweled harnesses in Principal Mathis's office. My stomach twisted into a sick knot.

"The *po-lice*," Elliot called over his shoulder. He pronounced the word carefully, as though he thought I might be having trouble hearing him. I wasn't. I was just breathing so hard that it was tough getting words out. Elliot was not breathing hard at all. He was probably fighting the urge to run circles around Sylvie and me.

Curse him and his long, basketball-trained, 100 percent human legs.

Neither Sylvie nor I answered him. He turned around so that he was jogging backward, facing us.

"We can call them anonymously," he suggested, looking quickly over his shoulder to make sure the path behind him was clear.

"And tell them *what*?" I demanded.

That many words at once took all the breath I had, and I had to pause to suck in enough air to keep from passing out. "That a Martian"—gulp—"is selling students"—gasp—"as pets"—gasp—"on Jupiter? No one will"—wheeze—"believe us!"

"No!" Sylvie sputtered. "You can't…"

She came to a halt, resting one hand on her knee and using the other one to motion us to stop. Her head hung down like a limp dish towel, and I could see sweat dripping in a steady trickle off the end of her nose.

Beside her, Elliot jogged uneasily in place.

"If Coach Carpenter catches us stopping, we'll have to do push-ups," he reminded us.

Sylvie grunted and waved her hand at him in what I had a feeling might be an obscene gesture on Mars.

I stopped too, gratefully, and took the opportunity to lift the end of my tail off the ground. It was all scraped up and raw. Even my newly formed calluses weren't enough to protect it from being dragged around on the ground this long. Maybe Coach Carpenter would let me stop running if I showed him *actual blood*…

Sylvie finally caught her breath and raised her head.

"You *can't* tell anybody about the Martian stuff!" she pleaded. "That was a secret!"

"We won't tell them about *you*," Elliot assured her. "Just Principal Mathis—"

"If they find out about her, they might find out about me. And then my mom would get in trouble. She might even lose her restaurant! And I'll get shipped back to Mars. Is that what you want?"

"I thought that was what *you* wanted," I reminded her. "At least, the going back to Mars part. You keep saying how your dad is coming to get you any day now—"

"He is," Sylvie snapped. "He *is* coming to get me."

"Then why do you care if you get sent back there?"

Sylvie removed a purple Pixy Stix from her pocket and tapped it thoughtfully against her lip.

"I *do* want to go back to Mars," she said finally. "But I don't want my mom to get in trouble."

"That's if they even *let* you go back," Elliot added helpfully. "In movies, whenever the government captures aliens, they do all kinds of experiments and stuff on them."

"Nobody," Sylvie said darkly, pointing her candy stick at Elliot, "is going to do experiments *on me*."

"Of course not," I agreed. "Obviously, we can't tell the police that Principal Mathis is a Martian. They'd never believe us anyway. We'll leave out all of the Mars and Jupiter stuff, and just tell them that we found a bunch of kids trapped in a portable. That's it. They don't have to know it has anything to do with aliens at all."

Sylvie shook her head. "When they find the kids, they'll arrest Principal Mathis. And once they arrest her, they'll find out she's a Martian. What if they start looking for other Martians? Allan was right, you know, I *am* an illegal alien. Just not exactly the way he thought," she added, with a slight smirk. "I mean, my mom's an American, so I guess that makes me an American too. But it's not like I have a social security number or a birth certificate or anything. My mom probably broke like half a dozen laws to smuggle me here!"

"Sylvie, we have to do something!" I exploded, although privately I was thinking about Mrs. Juarez and how nice she had been to me. I didn't want her to get in trouble or Sylvie to get taken away. But… "We can't let eleven kids get shipped off to Jupiter!"

Sam Ramsey had been kicked out just that morning, for hanging a "Beware of Dog" sign on the back of my chair (with "Dog" crossed out and "Dinosaur" handwritten in). We could only assume he had been put in the portable with the others. That brought the total number of expelled kids to eleven.

"She won't ship off *eleven* kids," Sylvie said. "The order was for thirteen, remember? And the order form said that 'delivery will be taken when all thirteen juveniles have been secured.' So she needs two more before she can deliver them. We've still got some time."

"Time to do what?" Elliot asked, still jogging in place. "You know, the rest of the class is going to catch up to us eventually and lap us…"

"Time to take care of this ourselves," Sylvie explained. "No police. *We'll* rescue everybody."

"How?" I demanded. "We can't get into the portable. We can't even talk to the kids inside—"

"Then what makes you think the police will be able to?" Sylvie said.

"The police can break down doors and stuff," I pointed out.

"So can *we*," Sylvie informed him. "If it comes to that. But I don't think it will. We just need some time to think and come up with a plan, OK?"

"I don't know…" I said. I thought about the kids in the porta-ble. Were they still running in mindless circles around the obstacle course? It seemed so wrong not to do something *immediately,* now that we knew.

Then again, I couldn't help but remember Parker's Butt Brain chant and Brad's face as he dumped water into my lap. Maybe a few days of them running the obstacle course wouldn't be the worst thing…

"The class is catching up!" Elliot announced, looking into the distance over our heads. "Quick! Someone pretend they hurt an ankle or something, so we don't get in trouble for stopping."

Sylvie immediately plopped down on the ground, and cradled her right foot in her hands. Elliot and I both bent down and pretended to help her.

"The Martian stuff is a secret," she told us, her voice barely over a whisper, even though Coach Carpenter and the rest of the class were still hundreds of yards away. "Humans aren't supposed to know *any* of it."

"Then why'd you tell us?" Elliot asked.

Sylvie looked up at him. There was hurt in her eyes.

"Because we're *friends*," she spat at him. "Friends tell each other secrets. Friends also *keep* each other's secrets."

Sylvie's chin wobbled, as though she were about to cry.

"OK, OK," I said quickly. "We won't tell the police. Or our parents. We'll figure this out ourselves. Right, Elliot?"

Elliot nodded and Sylvie's face lit up.

"Thanks, fellas," she said. "I knew I could count on you. We'll think of something. I'm sure of it."

But by the end of the day, none of us had had any bright ideas.

I regretted my promise to Sylvie for the entire walk home.

Well, not exactly *regret*. I was glad she had trusted Elliot and me with her secret, and I wanted to keep it for her. But that didn't change the fact that there were eleven kids who needed our help…

Eleven kids who tortured you. Bullied you. Threw rings at your plates.

I tried to ignore the nasty little voice in my head. The one that sort of wanted to see Parker and his cronies shipped off to Jupiter.

Let them all realize what happens when they pick on Sawyer Bronson!

I shook my head violently to silence the voice.

No matter what they had done to me, none of them deserved to be sold as pets on another planet. And if I was the only one (well, along with Elliot and Sylvie) who could do something about it, then I would. Because it was the right thing to do. I would think of something brilliant.

Any minute now…

I was almost beginning to wish I really did have a second brain in my butt.

No flashes of inspiration came to me, so I let myself into the

Cory Putman Oakes

house, waved to my mom, and went upstairs to begin the excruciat-
ing process of disinfecting the scrapes on my tail.

Half a bottle of Bactine later, I realized I should really ask my
grandfather if there was a less painful way to heal dinosaur skin…

My grandfather.

He was not the police and he was not a parent, so talking to
him wouldn't technically be breaking my promise to Sylvie. Plus,
he hadn't bothered to answer my last message, so he probably
wouldn't even read it. So what was the harm?

I finished up with the Bactine and sat down at my computer.

From: SBronson@jackjames.com
To: DrSteg@BCemail.com

Dear Grandpa,

I don't know if you got my last email or not, but I'm writing you
again because things have gotten weird. For one thing, my principal is an alien. And I think she might be evil. My new friend,
Sylvie, is an alien too. But she's not evil. (I think she's a different
kind of alien.)

I also think that a bunch of kids in my class might be in trouble.
Sylvie and my friend Elliot (he's not an alien or a dinosaur—he's
just a normal kid) and I are trying to help them, but we don't really
know what we're doing. Sylvie says we shouldn't talk to the police
or anyone else, but I'm not sure we can handle this on our own.

I don't know what aliens have to do with dinosaurs. Do you?

Maybe it's just a coincidence. It seems like there's a lot of weird stuff going on here, all at once.

Anyway, I'm really hoping to hear from you soon…

Love,
Sawyer

PS My tail is getting better, but it still really hurts when it gets scraped up. Is there any kind of special cure for dinosaur skin?

I sat there for ten minutes after I hit SEND, but nothing new popped up in my inbox.

With a sigh, I went downstairs to make myself a big salad and put the finishing touches on my science fair project.

19

12 Percent Dinosaur

One of the perks of being a walking, talking science experiment is that when forced to come up with an idea for my science fair project, I didn't really have to strain my brain too hard.

My project was titled "What Part of Me Is Dinosaur?" All I did was order an online DNA kit, rub a cotton swab on the inside of my cheek, and send it, along with a blood sample (courtesy of Dr. Gilmore), to the address on the box. Several weeks later, I received a computer printout of my "Whole Genome Test," which identified which of my genes could be classified as human and which were dinosaur.

My conclusion: I am approximately 12 percent dinosaur.

My dad helped me carry my foam board display into the school gym from the car. My mom followed, carrying a stuffed stegosaurus that she thought would look cute in front of my display.

The green plush creature had six fuzzy plates on its back and a stupid grin on its face. I had hidden it in the dryer earlier that day, hoping my mom would forget all about it. And she probably would have, if Fanny hadn't had an accident on the bath mat that afternoon, prompting an unscheduled load of laundry.

Whatever. I really could have cared less about my project or the fair in general. I just wanted to get it over with so that I could get back to trying to figure out what to do about Principal Mathis.

The gym was jam-packed with long folding tables, most of which were already occupied by a forest of foam core panels. A stage had been set up on the far wall, along with a microphone and a row of folding chairs.

"Sawyer! Over here!"

Elliot waved me over to a table that was near the stage and directly underneath one of the basketball hoops. He had probably picked the spot on purpose; his project was titled "The Physics of the Dunk." It featured a blurry picture of him dunking a basketball, plus a lot of measurements and equations.

"Quick," Elliot said, nodding to the empty spot beside his project. "Set yours up here. The judges are already making the rounds."

He pointed. A few tables away, Principal Mathis and a herd of teachers were making their way slowly toward us, stopping briefly in front of each project and jotting down notes on their clipboards.

My dad set my project on the table, while my mom fussed over how to arrange the stuffed dinosaur.

"Where's Sylvie?" I asked Elliot.

"Bathroom. With her mom." Elliot snickered and pointed to the project on the other side of his. "Get a load of *that*."

Sylvie's project was titled:

IS IT WORTH IT?

THE ENVIRONMENTAL IMPACT

OF ELEMENTARY SCHOOL SCIENCE FAIRS

Her conclusion:

No.

Number of public elementary schools in the US: 67,000

Average number of students per school: 400

Average number of foam core boards per science project: 2

= 53,600,000 sheets of nonbiodegradable polystyrene

in exchange for negligible educational benefit

"That Sylvia is quite a pip," said Mom, studying Sylvie's project over my shoulder. "She certainly has her own opinions, doesn't she?"

"Yes, she does," I agreed.

"WELCOME!"

The enthusiastic voice of Dr. Cook boomed out over the onstage microphone.

It was immediately followed by an earsplitting *SCCREEEEEE EEEEEEEE.*

"Ahhhhhh-*chooo*!"

Mr. Broome, who was wide-awake and therefore sneezing uncontrollably, jumped onto the stage and adjusted a knob on the speaker behind Dr. Cook.

"THAT'S BETTER!" Dr. Cook exclaimed, still yelling, despite the presence of the microphone. "WELCOME TO THE J.J. ELEMENTARY SCHOOL SCIENCE FAIR! JUDGING IS CURRENTLY UNDERWAY, AND WE WILL BE ANNOUNCING THE WINNERS WITHIN THE HOUR!"

"Pssst!"

I looked around, trying to pinpoint the source of the summons. Finally, I saw an orange sleeve waving at me impatiently from the other side of the table, behind Elliot's project.

"Pssst!" Sylvie said again. "Sawyer! Elliot! Get over here!"

I met Elliot's eyes, and we both glanced at our parents. They were busy greeting Mrs. Juarez and weren't paying any attention to us.

We slipped around the table. Sylvie held out a sheet of paper.

"A sixth grader handed me this when I came out of the bathroom," she said. Her face looked very serious.

The paper had the slightly blurry quality of a photocopy. The words got straight to the point:

THIS IS A SCHOOL. NOT A ZOO.
HUMANS ONLY.

If you agree, sign your name below and help us TAKE BACK OUR SCHOOL.

Megan O'Connell   ERNie Hobbs

Manny Ortega   Hannah Lee

Tyler Robinson

Eva Lewis

[When all signature lines are full, return this form in secret to Allan Huxley or Cecilia Craig.]

There were half a dozen signatures already, and room for at least half a dozen more. I didn't recognize the first few names, but the last two were kids I had known since kindergarten.

I felt like I had been punched in the stomach.

"We've got to tell Principal Mathis," Elliot said immediately.

Sylvie slapped him neatly upside the head.

"Ow! What was—"

"We can't tell her," I explained, as Sylvie snatched the paper from Elliot and crumpled it in her hand. "If we do, she'll have grounds to expel Allan and Cici. Then she'll have her last two, and she'll send all thirteen of them off to Jupiter!"

"Oh, right." Elliot frowned. "Well, what do we do?"

"There are more of these being passed around," Sylvie said. "We've got to find them before Principal Mathis sees them."

I looked over my shoulder at the tables across the aisle.

"You guys get on that," I said. "I'm going to go talk to Allan."

I grabbed the paper out of Sylvie's hand and marched over to Allan's table, trying to smooth out the crumples as I walked.

I don't know what came over me. It was a strange sense of courage. Or possibly anger. Or both. Whatever it was, it was a new sensation for me.

Allan saw me coming and raised his hands up in a gesture of innocence.

"Nothing personal, Butt Brain. This is about a safe and sanitary school environment."

I'll give you a safe and sanity environment, said my inner voice. *On Jupiter.*

"Allan," I said out loud, shoving my inner voice to the back of my brain. I held up the paper. "You've got to get rid of these. Hide them. Before Principal Mathis sees."

"I'm not scared of her," Allan sniffed, but not before he cast a wary eye around the gym. The judging had ended, and our principal, in all of her big-haired glory, was nowhere to be seen.

Cici came up to stand beside Allan. She was holding a huge pile of petitions in her hands. I couldn't tell if they had all been filled out or if they were more blank ones.

"Scared of who?" she asked.

"Mathis," Allan answered.

"Praying Mantis?" Cici mocked, and giggled. "What's the worst she could do? Expel us? Ha! At least we wouldn't have to look at Sawyer's ugly face anymore!"

"It's worse than that—" I started, then hesitated. Was there any chance I could make them understand without telling them the whole truth? "You just have to trust me. Do *not* give her a reason to expel you."

Cici scoffed. She handed Allan half of the petitions and turned away.

Allan looked down at the papers he was holding. Then he looked up at me, with a suddenly doubtful expression in his eyes.

I had his attention.

"Your name is on those," I pointed out. "All she has to do is find *one*, and she has everything she needs to nail you."

"So?" he demanded. "What do you care?"

"I don't," I told him. And I didn't. Not really. But there were eleven other kids who I hated a whole lot less than Allan, and their only hope was that Principal Mathis didn't find two more victims.

And here, Allan and Cici were offering themselves up on a silver platter.

"Just believe me," I implored. "I can't tell you everything. I wouldn't, even if I could. But trust me; it's worse than you could possibly imagine."

Allan hesitated and flipped through the papers in his hands.

"Why don't you just leave school?" he asked me. "You don't belong here. And now you're messing things up for the rest of us."

I narrowed my eyes at him, but the truth was, it's not like that thought hadn't occurred to me. Maybe I *didn't* belong in a human school anymore. But where would I go? There was no school for human-dino hybrids. And if there was, Elliot and Sylvie wouldn't be there. I'd have to be friends with the T. rex from Jersey.

"This is my school," I informed Allan. "If you don't like that, then why don't *you* leave?"

"I'm not the freak," Allan said coldly.

That word—*freak*—triggered something inside me. I felt it rise up, just like it had that day in the cafeteria. The day that I had roared. My hands started to shake. I felt a rumble somewhere deep in my insides. Like the growl of an empty stomach, only angrier.

I pressed my lips together, determined not to open them until I had gotten it together.

But before I could gather myself, a hand reached out and plucked the stack of petitions out of Allan's hands.

Principal Mathis adjusted her glasses and held the papers up until they were only about an inch away from the end of her nose.

"What have we here?"

It took Principal Mathis a few moments of fierce squinting to read the petition. Her eyes lingered near the bottom, where Allan's and Cici's names were spelled out, clear as day.

I could have sworn that the corners of her mouth twitched up into a smile, but it was only for a fraction of a second. Then the smile was replaced with the grim look of a no-nonsense educator who was being forced to do something unpleasant for a student's own good.

Standing this close to her, underneath the bright lights of the gym, it was more than obvious to me that her human face was nothing more than a mask. For one thing, there was a cluster of wrinkles near her ear, where the skin on the mask didn't quite match up with the skin on her real face. Elliot must have stretched out the mask when he was messing with it in her office.

How had nobody else ever noticed anything strange about her before?

"Do you have anything to say for yourself?" she asked Allan.

"N-no, ma'am," Allan stammered. He looked down at his feet, then back up at me.

There was real fear in his eyes. For all his bravado, he had believed me when I warned him not to let Principal Mathis catch him.

At least, he had believed me enough to be scared now that it had happened.

"Cici Craig!" Principal Mathis said loudly.

Half a table away, Cici turned around. She paled when she saw Mathis holding the petitions, but quickly turned on a look of defiance.

"Yes?" she said.

Mathis put a hand beneath Allan's elbow and guided him over toward Cici.

"I need to see you both in my office right away," she chirped, and steered them both toward the door of the gym.

"No, wait!" I stepped forward, and tried to plaster a giant smile on my face. "It was just a joke, Principal Mathis. I made the photocopies. Allan and Cici had nothing to do with it."

"Nice try, Sawyer," Principal Mathis said over her shoulder.

She did not stop leading Allan and Cici toward the door.

Desperate, I looked around for help. But there was none. The science fair was going on normally. Allan's and Cici's parents were several tables away, talking with Dr. Cook, completely oblivious to the fact that their children were being taken away, possibly forever. Even if they were to look up and see them walking away with Principal Mathis, they probably wouldn't think anything of it. They'd probably think their kids had won the science fair or something. They didn't know our principal was a vicious alien, bent on selling her students to a pet dealer on Jupiter.

A wave of panic washed over me. When Principal Mathis paused to open the wide double doors that led out of the gym, Allan looked over his shoulder at me; our eyes locked.

Sylvie and Elliot appeared at my side, just as the doors shut behind Principal Mathis and her two latest victims.

Neither of them said anything. But I knew they were thinking the same thing I was. Principal Mathis had her thirteen. There was no more time to waste. We *had* to do something.

But what?

20

Flan (And Other Bribery Techniques)

I didn't sleep much that night.

Allan, Cici, and their parents were still in Principal Mathis's office when the science fair ended. We had seen them in there from the parking lot, probably finalizing fake preparations to send them off to Camp Remorse.

Neither Elliot, Sylvie, nor I could think of a reasonable excuse to stick around school any later, so we'd had no choice but to get into our parents' cars and go home. Our only hope was that Principal Mathis would wait until morning to send everybody off to Jupiter. By morning, we would have a plan. By then, we would know exactly what to do.

But on the way to school the next morning, I had to admit I still had no idea what we were going to do. What *could* we do? Three kids, up against an evil Martian smuggler? Sure, one of us was half Martian. But I couldn't really see how that was going to help our odds.

I wanted to run to the portable first thing, to make sure the kids were still there. But instead, I headed for class. Maybe Elliot or Sylvie was there already. And maybe one of them had come up with a brilliant plan.

Elliot was there. But I could tell by the hopeful expression on his face when I walked in that he had also been counting on somebody else coming up with an idea.

"Nothing?" I asked him, feeling deflated.

"Zip," he said, sighing. He was sitting on top of his desk, holding his basketball in one hand and a Pop-Tart in the other.

"Maybe one of us should go to the portable," I suggested. "And see if they are even—"

"They're there," came Sylvie's voice.

She came bounding through the door behind me, twirling something red around her fingers.

"I just saw them in the portable, running the obstacle course. Right before I got my hands on *this*." She held up her hand, revealing a familiar red circle key chain.

My jaw dropped open.

"Mathis's key?" I exclaimed. "From your 'source' again? The same one who left the door open for us the night we broke into the school?"

Sylvie nodded. I took the key from her and studied the red disk. It looked like some sort of team logo, but not one I recognized. It was a picture of a large volcano. The lava spewing out of the top spelled out the name "Red Razers." At the base of the volcano was a flaming soccer ball and a warning to "Fear the Red."

"Soccer?" Elliot asked, looking over my shoulder. "Mathis likes soccer?"

Sylvie nodded. "It's kind of a big deal on Mars."

I handed her back the key chain.

"Sylvie," I said, "Elliot and I are not doing another thing until you tell us who your source is. Seriously, we deserve to know. Who keeps helping you?"

Sylvie hesitated for just a second and then shrugged.

"Ms. Helen," she admitted finally.

"Ms. Helen?" Elliot and I exclaimed together.

Sylvie nodded, looking fiercely proud of herself.

"Why would Ms. Helen do that?" I asked, confused, trying to picture the grumpy lady behind the fan going out of her way to do anything for anybody.

"Oh, she has her reasons," Sylvie said mysteriously. Then she smiled. "Plus, she *really* likes the flan from my mother's restaurant."

"Now that I believe," Elliot mumbled.

Sylvie wrapped her fingers around the key and kissed her knuckles. "Come on! Let's go!"

"Wait a sec," I said, thinking about something. "What about the electricity? Is the doorknob electrified again? If it is, and if we put a metal key into it, we're going to get electrocuted."

Sylvie reached into her backpack and pulled out a pair of heavy-duty work gloves.

"I stole these. From the janitor's closet down the hall. Did you know they don't even lock it? There's amazing stuff in there."

"What time did you get to school today?" I asked, incredulous.

Sylvie just smiled. "Come on! Before everyone else gets here."

She turned toward the door. I took a step to follow her, but Elliot, who had been mysteriously silent for the past couple of minutes, stayed where he was.

I threw him a questioning *are you coming?* look.

"I don't know," Elliot hedged. "First period is starting in a bit…"

Sylvie stomped her foot.

"This is *way* more important than first period, Elliot!"

"*Why?*" Elliot jumped off his desk, suddenly quite intent. "Why is it more important? Why do you care so much about saving those… those *bullies?*"

Sylvie looked momentarily startled, and I understood why. This was the first time Elliot had ever put his foot down to her. In fact, it was the first time I had seen him put his foot down to anybody in a long time.

Elliot pointed a finger in her direction. "You're not the only one who has been doing some thinking," he said. "You know what I've been thinking about? How those kids tortured me last year. And why? Because I got tall. I didn't want to be tall. I didn't ask to be tall. I just *am*."

Elliot slammed the basketball down at his feet. Sylvie and I both jumped. The ball bounced three times, then rolled behind him. He ignored it.

"They acted like I had committed some sort of horrible crime, even though it had nothing to do with them. You saw it, Sawyer!"

"I did," I admitted. I had. It was true. And yet…

"And this year they turned right around and did the same thing to

168

you!" Elliot continued. "They made you into a ring toss game! They told you, to your face, that you belong in a zoo instead of a school. And now you're willing to risk getting in all sorts of trouble to rescue them? *We* could end up getting shipped to Jupiter right along with them. Or at least, I could. I'm not a hybrid, like the two of you. Have either of you thought of that?"

I sighed and looked down at my feet. It was true, all of it. It was. And yet…

"Elliot," Sylvie spoke up. "Principal Mathis wants to *kidnap* them. To send them to another *planet*, where they'll never see their families again. I know they made you miserable, and I've seen them do the same to Sawyer. But do you really think they deserve what they're about to get?"

"If it was us in there," Elliot pressed her. "If it was you, me, and Sawyer, do you think Allan would lift a finger to help us? No way! He'd probably volunteer to stand guard to make sure Principal Mathis got away with it!"

"We don't know that," Sylvie argued.

"*I* do," Elliot told her. "And don't try to tell me you know humans better than I do. You're only half human. You've only been on Earth for like a month. You don't get it."

"I'm only half human too," I piped up. "Does that mean *I* don't get it?"

"You're different," Elliot sniffed, glaring at Sylvie.

"How?" I demanded. "How am I different?"

"You grew up here," Elliot growled. "You know those kids. You know they're never going to change. Once they're done making fun of you, they'll move on to some other kid. Then another kid, then another one, and so on. They don't deserve to be saved."

"Maybe not," I agreed. "But I'm going to do it anyway."

I took a step, one that brought me away from Elliot and closer to Sylvie. Sylvie gave me a grateful half smile.

Elliot's face fell.

"Come with us," I implored him.

He shook his head and bent to pick up his basketball.

"I'm staying here. If you end up as somebody's pet on Jupiter, don't say I didn't warn you."

21

Good Boys (and Girls)

As Sylvie and I raced for the portables, the bell signaling the beginning of first period rang behind us. We both picked up the pace. Ms. Filch usually took attendance in the first few minutes of class. Once she discovered we were missing, we wouldn't have much time before people came looking for us.

I wasn't sure if Elliot would even try to cover for us.

"Don't worry about Elliot," Sylvie said, jogging alongside me. "If we *do* end up on Jupiter, at least someone will know where we went!"

"We need a plan," I said, trying to black out all thoughts of Elliot and Jupiter. "How are we going to get everyone out of the portable?"

"I don't know." Sylvie shrugged and held the key up purposefully. "We'll have to see what happens once we get inside. Maybe they'll just follow us out!"

I remembered the blank expression on Brad's face when I had

seen him through the window. Something told me that it wasn't going to be that easy.

We reached the portable, and I immediately went around back to peek through the window. I believed Sylvie, of course. But I was still relieved to see for myself that all my former classmates were there, running the obstacle course just as they had been the other day.

When Brad ran by, I started counting.

1 bully, 2 bully, 3 bully…

"Why does their hair look all funny?" Sylvie asked, looking through the window as well.

4 bully, 5 bully, 6 bully, 7 bully…

"I don't know," I said impatiently. Honestly, that was such a *girl* thing to worry about at a time like this.

8 bully, 9 bully, 10 bully…

"I'm serious," she said. "It's like all weird and spiky."

*11 bully, 12 bully…*and then Brad came back around.

Wait. What? Brad had been bully #1.

"Sawyer," Sylvie said haughtily. "Are you even lis—"

"There's only twelve!" I exclaimed. "Twelve kids! Allan and Cici were supposed to make thirteen!"

"You must have counted wrong," Sylvie said, pulling out her notebook and opening to the first page. She counted quickly down her column of names. "Thirteen kids have been expelled. You must have just missed one."

I bit my lip. I was almost positive I hadn't missed anybody. But they had been running and jumping over things, so maybe Sylvie was right…

Anyway, that really didn't matter right now.

"Let's go," I said, tugging on the hood of her sweatshirt and gesturing for her to follow me back around to the front door. My hands were starting to shake. Something was going to happen when we opened that portable door. I wasn't sure exactly what, but it was definitely going to be—

"Ow!"

I gulped down a roar as I rounded the corner and ran right smack into a green Ducks jersey.

Elliot staggered backward and steadied himself by grabbing onto the side of the portable.

"What are *you* doing here?" Sylvie demanded.

Elliot shrugged, looking sheepish.

"When you weren't there for attendance, I told Ms. Filch you were both home sick. And then I figured as long as I was going to lie for you, I might as well help you. So here I am."

He held up the hall pass.

"I said I felt sick too, and I needed to go see the nurse. It'll be a while before Ms. Filch figures out I never made it there."

I was so glad to see him, I felt like hugging him.

But Sylvie beat me to it. She threw herself at Elliot, wrapping her orange-sweatshirted arms around his middle.

Elliot suffered through the hug, rolling his eyes at me as he did.

"Being the good guy really sucks, doesn't it?" I remarked.

"Totally," he said. But he was smiling.

We kept our eyes peeled for Principal Mathis, or anybody else, as we crept up to the door of the portable. But there was no one in sight.

With luck Ms. Filch wouldn't be able to sort out our various excuses for being absent until the end of the period. That should give us plenty of time to get our classmates out of the portable and safely to…

Where, exactly?

As Sylvie slipped on the janitor's oversized gloves, I realized we hadn't thought about what we were going to do once we had everyone out of the portable. Call the police? They'd have to believe us then, wouldn't they?

I guess we'd cross that bridge once we came to it.

Sylvie took a deep breath and shoved the metal key into the lock. There were no sparks this time, and the lock gave a sharp click as it opened. Sylvie opened the door triumphantly and let us all inside.

The front windows were boarded up, so there was not enough light to see anything. But then there was a hissing sound. Several hissing sounds. A puff of air hit my face, and there was a sickeningly sweet smell that made my nose wrinkle in disgust.

A crushing weight hit me as Elliot collapsed against my right side. I tried to hold him up and push him back onto his feet, but it was like trying to stand up a giant, wet noodle.

Then I was falling. And my eyes were closing. I let go of Elliot and we both toppled to the floor. I landed on top of a lump that was probably Sylvie. Then everything started spinning and went dark.

"Ridiculous. Absolutely, positively *ridiculous*."

I blinked. It was dark all around me, but I could see a thin line of light. And that seemed to be where the complaining was coming from.

"No respect for my time at all. I would expect this from a human. But a Jupiterian? They are supposed to be the ones with manners. *Honestly!*"

After a couple more blinks, I was reasonably sure the light was coming from underneath a door. The complainer was on the other side of the door.

And where was I? It felt small. Even though I couldn't see much, it had that closed-in feeling, like the walls were just inches away from me on all sides. I reached out a hand to check, only to discover that my hands were stuck behind me. I was tied up! My legs seemed to be tied up, too, because I couldn't move them very much.

"Hey!" I yelled. At least my mouth wasn't covered. "What's going on?"

The door opened immediately, spilling light into my prison. It *was* small. Nothing more than a closet, crammed full of art supplies. Several easels and a stack of construction paper had been shoved aside to make room on the floor for me. And for Sylvie, who lay blinking beside me.

We were both tied up with jump ropes.

Principal Mathis stood in front of us. At least, she was dressed like Principal Mathis. And she had Principal Mathis's poofy hair. And her glasses. But her human mask was missing.

Her face was the same shape as a human face. Her eyes, mouth, and nose were all in the right places. But her eyes were almost perfectly round, like quarters, behind her thick glasses. Her mouth was just a tiny line, and her ears were human-shaped but pressed flat against the sides of her head. Her skin looked smoother than human skin. And slightly pinker. I couldn't see her antennae, but they were probably still hidden in her tall hair. I wondered if she used clips, like Sylvie did.

Principal Mathis's tiny Martian lips curled up into a smile. Then she looked back over her shoulder at the clock on the wall.

"Eight forty-five a.m.," she said to herself, reading the clock. "Thirty minutes. Well, that's not too bad for just two sprays."

"What?" I asked, finally noticing that Principal Mathis was holding an aerosol can. It was the Good Boy spray, the stuff I had found in the cabinet the night we had broken into her office. I had assumed it was something for pets, but that was before I knew she considered humans to be pets...

"What is that stuff?" I asked.

There were probably more pressing questions I should have asked. *Why are we tied up?* and *Where is Elliot?* both came to mind, but all I could really focus on at that moment was the spray can.

Principal Mathis held up the can so I could see it better.

"This, Sawyer, is a valuable behavioral tool. Humans can be so stubborn, so unwilling to obey new masters. At least at first. I never place a pet with a new family without giving them a free can."

"What does it do?" I asked. Mostly because I had the feeling it had just been used on me.

"One puff in the face results in a calm, obedient human. When used properly, in conjunction with positive behavioral reinforcement, I find that it can help smooth over the adjustment period when a pet is introduced into a new home."

"'Good Boy'?" Sylvie read the label, and snorted. "*I'm* not a boy."

Principal Mathis waved her off.

"There's also a line of pink Good Girl sprays, for female pets. But the formulation is the same. Only the packaging is different. For marketing purposes, of course."

Sylvie sniffed, not bothering to respond. Principal Mathis continued. "The sprays are also excellent for training purposes. I've been using it here with great success."

She moved to the side of the door frame so that Sylvie and I could see behind her. She gestured to a fan in the corner of the room, up near the ceiling. Beside the fan was a can of Good Boy spray that had been rigged to spray every couple of seconds. The fan panned slowly from side to side, spreading the spray over the heads of the kids on the obstacle course below.

I was so focused on the fan that it took me a few seconds to realize that there was a new runner on the course.

Even from my place sprawled on the floor of the closet, it was easy to make out Elliot's lanky form swinging across the monkey bars.

"Elliot!" I yelled, struggling to sit up. "ELLLLLIIIIIIOOO OOTTTTT!"

"He can hear you," Principal Mathis assured me. "But he's been told not to respond. Like I said, the Good Boy spray results in near total obedience. Fascinating stuff, isn't it?"

"If it's so great, why didn't it work on us?" Sylvie demanded. "Sawyer and I aren't running your stupid obstacle course right now."

Principal Mathis held up the can again, and this time I noticed a familiar picture just underneath the Good Boy brand name. It was the two twisted ladders, the red one and the green one, from the Amalgam Labs movie. And underneath, there was a lot of fine print I couldn't read from where I was sitting.

"One puff produces compliance. That's all I used on Elliot. Two or more puffs in the face results in unconsciousness, which is what I did to you and Sawyer. I advise my clients to use multiple puffs sparingly, as it tends to interfere with the bonding process. As a general rule, I use two puffs only as a last resort, usually when a pet's behavior has created a safety concern."

She set the can down on the floor and bent down, so that she was looking us both right in the face.

"And let me be frank. Your recent behavior has created a *serious* safety concern."

"We're not pets," I told her, trying in vain to free my hands. Unfortunately, the jump ropes were quite strong and were doing their job well.

"Oh, I agree." Principal Mathis nodded, setting down the can and standing back up again. "I rarely place hybrids anymore. I've found them to be too dangerous. Hybrids are a lucrative market, but there's far too much liability for my taste."

I looked uneasily at Sylvie. My dinosaur parts marked me as an obvious hybrid. But besides Elliot and me, everyone believed Sylvie was fully human. Or so we had thought…

"How did you know?" Sylvie asked Mathis.

Our principal rolled her eyes. "Oh, please, my dear. Your hair alone practically *screams* Martian. I'm shocked the Martian Council is letting you run around on Earth with your Martian-ness so poorly concealed. Especially given who your father is. I can't imagine how he can be allowing this."

"Your father?" I asked Sylvie. "I thought he was a restaurateur?"

"Among other things," Sylvie mumbled, glaring up at Principal Mathis.

She smiled in response and gathered up her purse.

"Fortunately, you will not be my problem for much longer. My client is running a little late, but they should be here to pick up their shipment within the hour."

"The Jupiterians?" I asked, alarmed. "They're coming *here*?"

"Yes. Soon. And after that, I will be free to move on."

She pulled what looked like a handful of skin out of her purse. She removed her thick glasses and turned away for a moment.

"You just go from school to school, pretending to be a principal and stealing kids?" I asked incredulously. "How could you?"

Principal Mathis turned back toward me. Now that she was wearing her human face, I forgot for a moment that she was a Martian. A crazy Martian, at that. All I could see now was the person who had promised me she would help me. The person I thought had been on my side.

And for a second, I think Principal Mathis remembered that person too. Her face softened, and she looked at me the way she had looked at me across the principal's desk when I had first met her.

"I never take the good ones, Sawyer. Only the troublemakers. The ones who make school miserable for everybody else. There were a lot of them here. Usually, I have to go to two or three schools to fill an order as large as this one. Think of it as a cleansing.

You may not realize it now, but what I have done here will only enhance your educational experience."

Her soft face melted, and her eyes became steely once more behind her enormous glasses.

"Of course, I am breaking the rules just a little bit today. I need thirteen to fill this order. As of this morning, I was one short. But my clients are eager to take possession of their shipment, and fortunately number thirteen fell into my lap just now."

I shook my head.

"You might need a lesson in math, Principal Mathis. You had thirteen last night," I argued. "Counting Allan and Cici, you expelled thirteen kids."

"Yes, I expelled thirteen. But one boy turned down my invitation to Camp Remorse."

My mind was racing. That *would* explain why I had counted only twelve. But who was missing? I wracked my brain. Who hadn't I seen on the obstacle course?

In my head, I ran through the list of expelled students. Gary, Brad, Mary, Nora, and Vivian had been expelled in the Purge. Jeremy and Emma, the next day. Then Justin and Gabrielle, for throwing food at me in the cafeteria. Then Sam, for hanging the sign on my chair. I had definitely seen all of them on the obstacle course. Who was I missing?

The answer came to mc suddenly: Parker.

It had been his disappearance that had caused us to go searching in the first place, but had we actually *seen* Parker in the portable, or had we just assumed he was there because all of the other kids were there? What had happened to Parker?

And more importantly, if Principal Mathis only had twelve...

I looked up. Mathis had been watching me work through all this in my head. She nodded when she realized I had finally caught up.

"Elliot brings the total up to thirteen," she explained. "Lucky for me he was with you this morning."

The sound of Elliot's name made me want to leap at Principal Mathis, but I was held back by the jump rope. I strained my arms as hard as I could, but nothing happened. Next to me, Sylvie was jerking back and forth, trying to free herself.

"You can't take him!" I yelled. "Elliot is one of the good ones! The best ones! You said it yourself, you never take the good ones!"

"Desperate times..." Principal Mathis shook her head and picked up the Good Boy spray. "He'll make someone an excellent pet. Don't you worry, I'll make sure he goes to a good family. Maybe even one with children for him to play with."

She took a step toward us, holding up the spray can.

"Now, time for you to go back to sleep. When you wake up, this will all be over."

"You won't get away with this!" Sylvie screamed at her. "We'll tell! I'll tell my father. And the police! And—"

Principal Mathis cut her off with a laugh that was more like a snort.

"I have never been afraid of the Martian Council. They have known about me for years, and they haven't been able to stop me yet. And as for the humans? Well, that's the wonderful thing about doing business on Earth. No one believes children. Not even when they're telling the truth."

She took a step closer to our closet. Then she smiled and held up the can, finger poised over the sprayer.

Next to me, Sylvie drew in a breath and held it, so that her cheeks puffed out. I did the same. No way was I breathing in any more of that stupid Good Boy spray. By the time we woke up this time, everyone would be gone. Including Elliot.

And Principal Mathis was right. No one would believe us.

Unfortunately, the decision not to breathe was not exactly a long-term solution to our problem. My lungs started to burn after about a minute. Beside me, I heard Sylvie pound the ground in frustration.

Principal Mathis stood patiently in front of us, holding the can at the ready. She wasn't the least bit concerned. She knew we would have to breathe eventually.

Sylvie gave in first. When she tried to get in a quick gasp of air, Principal Mathis sprang forward like a cat and blasted her in the face with the Good Boy spray. Four times.

Sylvie's eyes grew wide. Then they rolled up into her head as she slumped to the floor.

I could smell the gross, sweet smell of the spray. That meant it was getting in through my nose. I couldn't help it—my hands were tied, so I couldn't use them to cover my nostrils.

I could feel my resolve crumbling. My anger toward Principal Mathis faded away as the Good Boy spray snuck up my nose and into my brain. I couldn't remember why I was upset. I only wanted to be good. I wanted her praise more than I wanted anything else in the world.

Principal Mathis leaned over me.

"Breathe, Sawyer," she ordered me.

I did. And my reward was four puffs of spray in the face.

Then there was just darkness.

22

One Fried Martian

Wake up! Sawyer! Wake up!"

An annoying voice was coming at me through a thick fog. I couldn't quite place who it was or what they were saying. Or why they wouldn't leave me alone.

"WAKE. UP!"

This time, the words were punctuated by a sharp pain in my right side. Then another one. And another one, and another one, as something kept hitting me mercilessly.

"Wake up! Wake up! Wake up! Wake up! Wake—"

"OK!"

My eyes flew open, and I rolled slightly to the side, to get out of the range of Sylvie's foot.

"What time is it?" I asked immediately. "Are we too late?"

"I don't know," Sylvie said. She sounded frustrated. I couldn't see her very well in the dim light of the closet. "I woke up a few minutes ago. It sounds really quiet out there…"

She trailed off.

We were probably too late.

Not that it really mattered. We were both still tied up in jump ropes and stuck inside a dark closet in a building everybody thought was abandoned. It could be hours before anybody found us. Maybe even days.

By then, it would be far too late to help Elliot.

My tail started to cramp. I had rolled over halfway on top of it. I shifted my weight, and it gave an involuntary jerk of relief. One of my tennis balls snagged something on a nearby shelf, causing a waterfall of what felt like construction paper to rain down on me.

Tennis balls.

"Sylvie!" I rocked upward to a sitting position. "See if you can use your feet to curl my tail up, so that the end is up by my hands."

"Why? Do you have an itch?"

"No, I have razor sharp spikes that can totally cut through jump rope."

I had spent so much time and energy trying to fit in, trying to convince everyone that I was safe to be around, that I had actually forgotten I could be dangerous.

When I wanted to be.

I could hear Sylvie wiggling around on the floor. After a moment, I felt her feet nudging the end of my tail toward my butt. It took a few more minutes, and a lot of grunting and weird contortions on both of our parts, but eventually I was able to get one of my spikes up to my bound hands. I twisted the tennis ball off the end and gingerly positioned a part of the rope against the sharp, serrated surface. I moved my hands back and forth a couple of times, and the spike sawed right through the rope.

Once my hands were free, I was able to cut myself and Sylvie out of our ropes in less than a minute. We threw ourselves against the closet door, but it flew open the second we touched it.

Principal Mathis hadn't even bothered to lock us in.

The kids were still running the obstacle course. I breathed a huge sigh of relief.

Above their heads, the clock said 9:02 a.m.

We had only been asleep for about ten minutes.

I looked at Sylvie in confusion.

She reached down and picked up the can of Good Boy spray, which Principal Mathis had left on the floor just outside of our closet.

"'Good Boy and Good Girl products have not been tested on hybrids,'" she read out loud. "'Results may be unpredictable.'"

I frowned. "Principal Mathis didn't know that?"

Sylvie shrugged. "She's a full-blooded Martian. Her vision is so bad she can probably barely see the can, let alone read the fine print. Come on, let's get everybody out of here before she comes back."

"And before the Jupiterians arrive," I added. I had absolutely no interest in meeting them.

Sylvie ran into the midst of the obstacle course.

"Hey!" she said, waving her hands to get everybody's attention. "It's OK! We're going to get out of here! Follow me!"

Everybody ignored her and continued along the course as though Sylvie wasn't there at all.

"Stop running!" Sylvie yelled at the top of her lungs. "Stop doing that! Did you hear me? We've got to get out of here!"

She marched over to Elliot and grabbed his arm.

He shook her off and leaped over a stack of mats without missing a beat.

"The fan!" I remembered suddenly.

I dragged a chair over to the corner. Standing on tiptoe, I was just barely able to reach the off button.

By the time I climbed down off the chair, the temperature in the room had already started to rise. The crazy obstacle course running continued for several minutes, but soon a few of the kids started to miss steps. A couple rubbed their eyes. Nora fell off the top of the climbing wall right onto Brad, who was stumbling around in a daze.

Allan locked eyes with me, and I could literally see the moment when the Good Boy spray left his system. One second his eyes were cloudy and unfocused. The next, they were piercing into me like twin laser beams.

With a snarl, Allan threw himself at me.

We fell to the floor in a tangle of arms and my tail. I thrashed, but Allan was much bigger than I was and I couldn't get him to budge. I squirmed as hard as I could, but Allan quickly had both of my arms pinned down to my sides. He was sitting on my chest, and my plates on my back were being squashed so painfully against the ground that it was hard for me to think of anything else.

Allan grinned down at me as he slowly pulled back his right arm, aiming a fist right at my face.

It occurred to me then that one of my tail spikes was still un-tennis-balled. And it could saw through Allan's leg just as easily as it had sawed through the jump rope.

No. That would just be proving Allan right. And there was no way I was going to do that.

I closed my eyes, bracing myself as I waited for the punch to land.

Then, suddenly, I heard Allan shriek. And the pressure on my chest was gone.

I opened one eye just in time to see Elliot pull Allan off me and set him roughly back down on his feet.

"I am twice your size," Elliot growled, keeping a grip on the front of Allan's T-shirt. "I could *break* you. And I will, if you ever mess with Sawyer again. Got it?"

Allan nodded quickly. Elliot released him but continued to glare threateningly at him.

Sylvie sauntered over, reading from the fine print of the Good Boy can again.

"'Abrupt cessation of product may cause violent outbursts in up to five percent of subjects,'" she quoted. She looked around suspiciously at the other kids.

None of the rest of them appeared to be part of the 5 percent. In fact, they all looked a little bit confused and out of it.

Allan smoothed down the front of his shirt.

"Sorry," he said to Elliot, then turned to me.

"Sorry," he repeated.

Elliot was looking at him strangely. The scary look on his face had been replaced by confusion.

"Dude? What's wrong with your hair?"

Allan brought a cautious hand up to his head. I had been concentrating so hard on the fact that he was about to punch me, I hadn't noticed that his usual buzz cut had been replaced by a full head of hair that was gelled into tall spikes.

"Mathis," he muttered, trying to make the spikes lay flat with the palm of his hand. Despite his efforts, the gel kept them more or less upright. "After she brought Cici and me here last night, she brought in a groomer. I think she gave me hair extensions."

"A *groomer*?" Sylvie exclaimed. I could have sworn she was holding back a giggle. I didn't blame her. The idea of Allan having his hair done like a poodle *was* pretty funny.

Allan shrugged.

"It's all pretty foggy. What exactly is going on?"

"We'll explain later," Sylvie said, before Elliot or I could open our mouths. "But right now, we've got to get out of here. Follow me!"

She strode purposefully toward the front door of the portable, putting on the heavy gloves she had snagged from the janitor's closet that morning. Most of the kids stumbled automatically after her. After being under the influence of Good Boy for so long, they were probably all a little more susceptible to being bossed around than usual.

"Are you OK?" Elliot asked me.

I nodded.

"Thanks," I told him. "I didn't know you could…I mean, I know you're tall and everything—"

"I always wanted to do that to Allan," he confessed with a smirk. "I just never got the nerve up."

Allan, listening to our conversation, just grunted. Then he turned toward the front of the room with everybody else.

Sylvie reached for the door. The second her gloved hand touched it, there was an enormous spark and she let out a high-pitched scream and flew backward.

For a moment she seemed to float in the air, moving in slow motion. Then she hit the ground on her back, with a painful sounding thud. She did not move.

And all of us smelled burned hair.

23

Nobody Here but Us Hybrids

Sylvie had already opened her eyes before any of us could reach her. A couple of wisps of smoke came from her toasted hair. There was only about half as many curls as there had been a moment ago, and the ones that were left were standing on end even more than usual.

But it was short enough now that the tops of her pink antennae were clearly visible, standing up amid the frizzy, smoking strands. Her hair clips must have melted.

Sylvie reached up to the top of her head, felt her antennae, and froze.

Everyone else froze too. For a long moment, we all just stared at her.

Allan was the first to speak. "Somebody had better explain what in the *blazes* is going on here!"

Ignoring him, Sylvie picked herself up off the ground and addressed Elliot and me.

"Let's try the windows," she suggested.

The front windows were boarded up. I headed for the ones in the back. Instead of touching them, I picked up a nearby chair and tossed it.

I braced myself for a shower of broken glass, but it never came.

The chair set off a shower of sparks when it got near the window, but bounced harmlessly off the glass and fell to the floor.

"Do you think the whole room is electrified on the inside?" Elliot asked. When no one answered him, he headed over to a rack of lacrosse sticks and picked them up one by one, studying them carefully.

"What is going on?" Allan asked again. He seemed to be speaking for the twelve would-be pets who were now huddled in the middle of the portable, carefully avoiding contact with the walls.

"Well," Sylvie said, with remarkable poise given that her entire right side was twitching a little bit. "There is a long version and a short version of the story. Which would you like?"

"The one that explains what is growing out of your head," Allan said. The usual attitude in his voice was now buried beneath a healthy amount of hysteria. "Are you, like, a Martian?"

Sylvie nodded.

Allan glanced over at Cici, who glanced over at Nora, who nodded.

"A few of us think Mathis is a Martian too," Allan told us.

"She is," I said. "And she's been keeping you here because she plans to sell you. As pets."

"Yeah, we figured that out too," Cici said. Like Allan, she was a pale shadow of her usual snarky self. Her long brown hair had been shaved on the sides, and the top portion was curled up in elaborate

192

loops. She had unraveled one loop and was twisting it nervously around her finger, again and again.

"Mathis's clients—the ones who want to buy you—are on their way," I said. "If we don't figure out a way to get you out of here, you're all going to end up on Jupiter."

Allan's head snapped up.

"Us?" he asked. "What about you?"

"Jupiterians don't like hybrids," I explained.

He nodded toward Sylvie.

"What about her? They don't want Martians either?"

"I'm only half Martian," Sylvie informed him. "They don't want me either."

"Bad news," Elliot interrupted, coming up behind us and gesturing to the walls. While we had been talking, he had used the metal handle of a lacrosse stick to systematically test the electric barrier. He had wrapped a towel around the end he was holding, but his hair was still sticking up a bit more than usual.

"The whole portable is electrified," he reported. Then, stating the obvious, "We're trapped."

Allan started pacing in an uneasy circle.

"I'm not just going to sit here and wait to get hit with more of that spray!" he growled.

"We'll think of something," I said, trying to calm him down.

"Easy for you to say," he snapped. "They don't want dinosaurs! *You're* not going to have to play fetch with some family on Jupiter!"

Allan and the others were all staring at me. And not like they usually stared at me, to get a glimpse of the freak show. For the first time, they were looking at me with something that looked a lot like…jealousy.

Actually, it looked *exactly* like jealousy. Even Elliot was eyeing my plates with a sort of wistful gleam in his eye.

All of a sudden, I realized something. Totally by accident, I had finally achieved what my father had advised me to do on the first day of school.

I had made all of the kids in my class wish that they had plates and a tail.

And just like that, a plan began to form.

"Hurry," Sylvie urged us all a short time later. "Mathis and her clients should be here any minute now!"

"We're almost done," Elliot assured her, cutting through four sheets of construction paper at once with the one and only pair of scissors we had found in the supply closet. "Is there any more tape?"

"I found some!" Gabrielle called, tossing it to him from the closet.

"Good!" Elliot yelled back, catching the tape neatly in one hand and handing it to Mary, who was busily taping papers to Sam's back. "See if there's any more paper. Color doesn't matter, does it, Sawyer?"

I thought for a second.

"I don't think so," I said finally. "Especially if it's all we've got."

Elliot nodded and went back to cutting.

I let out a quick breath and looked nervously around the room. It wasn't every day you saw fourteen kids, all hard at work, executing a plan you yourself had come up with. At least, it wasn't every day for me.

I was starting to get nervous that it wasn't really going to work.

I felt a hand on my shoulder, and I jumped a mile before I looked over and saw it was Allan.

When I realized it was him, I jumped another mile.

He took his hand off my shoulder and raised both hands above his head.

"I come in peace, OK?" he said.

I bit back a smile at his oddly appropriate choice of words. I think Allan realized what he had said too; the corners of his mouth went up a fraction of an inch as he lowered his arms back down.

"You look like you're thinking about something," he prompted me.

I nodded.

"Before she left, Mathis told me that Parker didn't accept her invitation to Camp Remorse," I told him. "Which is why Parker isn't here. But he's not at his house. And you said you couldn't find him either. So…where is he?"

"Oh." Allan shifted his weight a bit uncomfortably. "Parker's at military school in Maryland."

"What?" I asked, incredulous.

Allan looked a tad embarrassed. "His mom told my mom a couple of days ago."

"Military school," I said thoughtfully. "Where they have to wear uniforms, right?"

Allan shrugged. "I guess so."

At least that explained why Parker's mom would throw out his clothes.

"Well, I guess I didn't eat him then," I said pointedly.

"I guess not," Allan said sheepishly.

There was a moment of awkward silence before Allan spoke again. "I've been thinking too," he announced.

"Really?" That must be new and different for him.

"Last night at the science fair," he began. "You tried to stop Mathis from taking me and Cici. And now you're here, even though the...the, Jupiter people don't want dinosaur pets."

He frowned and trailed off, apparently having lost the thought that had been about to occur to him.

"Yeah..." I encouraged him.

"Why?" he asked. "Why are you helping us? After everything that we—I—have done to you?"

I bit my lip and thought about it. I examined Allan's face while I did. He wasn't being smart, or mean, or jerkish. He really wanted to know the answer. He truly could not understand what I was doing here. Was that because it would never have occurred to him to go out on a limb to help someone else? Or maybe because no one had ever done something like that for him?

It was food for thought. Some other time when Jupiterians weren't about to descend on us and try to kidnap my best friend.

"I don't know, Allan," I said finally. "Maybe the brain in my butt has finally taken over the brain in my head."

Allan smiled. It was kind of a frightening thing, to see his face squint up like that beneath his oversized forehead. It looked especially weird with his insane, spiky hair. And at the same time, it was the least scary he had ever looked to me.

"Yeah," he said slowly, as his grin widened. "That must be it."

Suddenly, the ground started shaking beneath us and there was a loud sound from outside, like a jet engine coming in for a landing.

"They're coming!" Sylvie yelled suddenly, backing away from the crack in the board that was nailed against the front window. "Places!"

Allan nodded at me, then fell back to stand beside Cici.

I took my place in the front of the room, just as Sylvie used the wooden handle of a broomstick to kill the lights.

Take me to your leader.

Any minute now, a Jupiterian was going to ask that. And when they did, he—she? it?—would be brought straight to me.

Why the heck hadn't I come up with a better plan?

A little bit of light came into the portable when Principal Mathis opened the door, but not much. It was barely enough for me to see the outline of our principal's hand, holding a can of Good Boy (or maybe it was Good Girl? It was too dark to see the color of the can) at the ready. And there was also enough light to see the slim outline of a broomstick knock the can out of her hand.

"Oh!" Principal Mathis exclaimed.

The lights flicked back on, just in time to catch Mathis on her hands and knees, fumbling around for the spray.

"Good afternoon, Principal Mathis," Sylvie said, nudging the can out of the way with one foot and bowing deeply. She purposefully made her voice sound toneless and distant, as though she were under the influence of the spray. "We are all ready to go, just like you asked."

Principal Mathis gaped at her. Forgetting about the can, which had rolled back behind my feet, she stood up slowly. She took off her thick glasses, quickly cleaned both lenses, then put them back on to gape at Sylvie some more.

"What happened to you?" she asked.

Sylvie smiled and patted the construction paper cape of plates she had taped to her back. She turned around slowly, making a full circle, to show off her long paper tail.

"Oh, nothing. Just a bit of grooming. I wanted to fit in with everybody else."

Principal Mathis glanced up and got a good look at the rest of us. Her mouth fell open.

There was an impatient sound from behind her. Like someone clearing their throat.

Principal Mathis's expression changed from confused to furious in approximately two seconds flat.

"Ladies and gentlemen," she began. "I'm not sure we need to—"

"Let us *see* them already!" an excited voice squealed. A tall, slim shape shoved Principal Mathis out of the way and walked eagerly into the room. A half dozen even taller figures followed the first, until the doorway was crowded with Jupiterians, and Principal Mathis was shoved, protesting, into the corner.

The Jupiterians were all about two feet taller than Principal Mathis. Their long robes were the same shiny silver as their skin, and their long arms and legs looked even skinnier than Elliot's. They all had tiny facial features that were squished into the middle of their faces, slits for eyes, tiny bumps for noses, and mouths that were even smaller than the thin line behind Mathis's human mask.

I heard someone behind me, probably Cici, gasp. But other than that, we all just stared silently at the Jupiterians while they stared back at us.

As mesmerized as we all were by them, I can only imagine how fascinating *we* must have looked to *them*. And how confusing.

Fifteen kids with dinosaur plates from their necks all the way down their backs. Right to the tips of their long tails.

Well, actually, we hadn't been able to find enough construction paper to make tails for everybody. But we directed Gary, Gabrielle, and Jeremy (the three kids without tails) to stand in the back. After all, Sylvie had said that *the only people who have worse eyesight than Martians are the Jupiterians*. Hopefully, she was right about that.

"Oh *no*," the first Jupiterian, the one who had pushed Principal Mathis out of the way, exclaimed. "Oh, Mathilda. This is quite wrong. This is absolutely *not* what we ordered."

The Jupiterian's voice was sort of singsongy. It sounded like a girl's voice, but all the Jupiterians had shiny bald heads and were dressed exactly the same, so I wasn't sure what gender any of them were. Or if the Jupiterians even had genders…

"I assure you, this is not what it appears to be," Principal Mathis rushed to explain. "These little rascals are just playing a prank on us. The thirteen I selected for you are all purebred human. These are just costumes."

"Costumes?" said a second Jupiterian. This one was the tallest of the group. His voice sounded male. And very ticked off.

"Yes, costumes. Construction paper and whatnot." Principal Mathis waved her hand carelessly in the air and let out the fakest laugh I have ever heard. "They're a spirited bunch, aren't they?"

The two Jupiterians who had spoken exchanged uneasy looks.

"I'll prove it to you," Principal Mathis offered. She raised a hand and stepped forward toward Sylvie.

I leaped forward and ducked underneath her hand, putting myself between her and Sylvie. Instead of hitting construction paper, her fingers fell onto my all-too-real plates. And they did not come off when she pulled.

"Purrrrrrr," I said, smirking at her. "Purrrrrr!"

She grabbed my topmost plate and shoved me away in disgust.

The Jupiterians let out a collective gasp of shock.

"Well, *this one* is real," Mathis admitted, looking embarrassed. "But I swear to you that the others are all—"

"Our order was quite specific," the first Jupiterian informed Mathis angrily. "Purebred humans. *No* hybrids. Particularly not dinosaur-human hybrids. That breed simply does not sell on our planet."

"I think we've seen enough," the tallest Jupiterian said. He turned to leave, and the others turned to follow him.

"Wait!" Principal Mathis exclaimed. She wrung her hands desperately. "I can explain!"

"Stop wasting our time," the tall Jupiterian hissed. When he turned to stare down at Principal Mathis, there were spots of red pulsating at both of his temples, just above where his ears should have been.

I had never seen a furious Jupiterian before. But I was pretty sure I was looking at one now.

"I am shocked that you would try to put one over on us, Mathilda," he said angrily. "I can promise you right here and now that we will *never* do business with you again. And we will be spreading the word that you took advantage of our diminished sight on this planet. You of all people should know how shameful it is to exploit someone's handicap!"

He strode purposefully out the door. The other Jupiterians followed him, all except for the first Jupiterian, the one I was pretty sure was a girl. She lingered at the door and looked sadly over her shoulder at us.

"You poor things," she said. "I do hope you all find happy homes."

Then the door slammed behind her, and the fifteen of us were left alone in the portable, facing a very, *very* angry Martian.

"You!" Principal Mathis pointed at me. "This was all your doing! Fine thanks I get for protecting you! I could have made a fortune with you on Mercury!"

Mercury?

Suddenly, I had really had enough of Principal Mathis.

I took a step backward and nearly tripped over the can of spray that Sylvie had kicked earlier. Now that the lights were on, I could see that it was labeled Good Girl in bold, pink letters.

Principal Mathis gave an angry growl and advanced on me.

I leaned down, picked up the can, and let loose four quick bursts of spray directly into her face.

Our principal fell to the ground like a stone. She hit the floor face-first, and half of her human mask stuck to the carpet and got scraped away as she rolled onto her side.

I reached down and patted her on the head.

"Good girl, *Mathilda*. Good girl."

Sylvie and Cici both giggled.

Before anyone could say anything else, there was the same jet-enginey sound from outside and a sudden, giant whoosh of wind. The door flew open, and six people in bright yellow jumpsuits charged in.

The Worst Kept
Secret On Earth

Do you know what is going to happen to Principal Mathis?"
I asked.

My grandfather set down his salad fork and wiped a smear of
dressing off his upper lip.

He nodded meaningfully toward the door of the kitchen, where
my parents had just disappeared. He put a finger to his lips and waited
a long minute, probably to make sure they really were, in fact, leaving
us alone with our salads to talk, like they had said.

It had been over six hours since the Jupiterians left and the team
from Amalgam Labs, led by my grandfather, had arrived. But it had
been a crazy six hours.

First, half of the team from the lab interviewed us, while the
other half ran an enormous thing that looked like a vacuum all
around the portable. Then, all of the scientists exchanged their
jumpsuits for civilian clothing and returned the twelve would-be

pets to their parents. Each parent was presented with a (fake) certificate of completion from Camp Remorse and assured that their child would be welcomed back at school the following Monday by Principal Kline.

Who, as it turned out, had not won the lottery after all, but had instead been the victim of a vicious prank by Principal Mathis. He had been campaigning for his job back ever since. The school board had been only too happy to reinstate him, given the vacancy created by Principal Mathis's abrupt departure.

Just hours after the incident, the school board had released a statement, praising the Portland FBI for capturing one Mathilda Mathis, a criminal wanted in twelve states for child abduction. The statement went on to say that Mathis would be taken to California, where she would stand trial for her crimes.

But I knew that wasn't really what was going to happen.

"Is it her?" my grandfather had asked one of the other scientists, as they both stood over Principal Mathis's unconscious body.

The other scientist, who actually looked a lot like Dr. Dana (from the movie), bent down and unfastened a clip from Principal Mathis's poofy hair.

One pink antennae sprang up from the top of her head.

The Dr. Dana look-alike felt around on the top of Mathis's head, searching for another clip. When she didn't find one, she sat back on her heels and nodded up at my grandfather.

"She has the birth defect, all right. The rarest on Mars. Yeah, this must be her."

Principal Mathis had only one antenna?

Maybe she *did* know a little something about being teased for looking different after all.

When the only sound from the kitchen was the washing of dishes and my parents talking, my grandfather finally sat forward in his chair to answer my question.

"Amalgam Labs will turn Principal Mathis over to the Martian authorities," he told me. "They'll have to decide what planet will put her on trial. It'll be a tough decision. She is wanted on at least seven of them, for one crime or another. Why do you ask?"

I shrugged and speared a forkful of lettuce sprinkled with my favorite vinaigrette.

"Just curious, I guess," I said, stuffing the lettuce into my mouth. With my mouth full, I had a moment to think before my next question.

Thanks to the Good Boy/Girl spray, most of the kids who had been in the portable had only hazy memories of any alien involvement in their kidnapping. And any wild stories they might tell later about Martian principals or Jupiterian pet dealers would be chalked up to post-traumatic stress disorder, overactive imaginations, or (as Principal Mathis had been counting on) simply being a kid.

This, according to my grandfather, was the way things had always been done.

Over dinner, he had explained things to my parents. He hadn't told them everything, of course. Just enough so I wouldn't be grounded for skipping out on school that day.

But now that it was just me and my grandfather, sitting alone in

205

my living room, I could finally get real answers to my questions. And I had *a lot* of them.

"I thought Amalgam Labs was closed in the United States," I began. "They said so in the movie we watched on the first day of school."

My grandfather rolled his eyes. He was still pretty young looking, as far as grandfathers go. And he didn't look anything like Dr. Cook, the only other scientist I knew. My grandfather looked like more of an Indiana Jones type of scientist, kind of rugged and windswept. He still had almost all his hair, and there were large patches of gray above his ears.

But not a single plate. Or even a hint of a tail.

"Oh, that movie," he said, shaking his head. "The lawyers made us put that together. You're right that we no longer have a facility in the U.S. But the United States government is actually one of our biggest supporters. A lot of the work we do involves alien technology. We employ more extraterrestrials than any other company on Earth."

"And are there, um, a lot of aliens on Earth?"

My grandfather gave me a secretive smile.

"The existence of extraterrestrials is the worst kept secret on Earth," he explained. "The United States, like every other country, officially denies that they have proof of alien life, even though they now have treaties with every planet in our solar system. A large number of aliens immigrate to Earth, even though they must live here in secret. Most of them work in places like Amalgam Labs, to improve human technology."

"Is that how they created the dinosaur gene?" I asked.

My grandfather nodded.

"Actually, it takes more than one gene for a human to develop dinosaur traits. Several thousand, in fact. We got them from the Saturians."

"Saturians?" I repeated. "You mean, like, from Saturn?"

"Yes. Dinosaurs still exist in the wild there," he said with a totally straight face. I marveled at this for a moment, but then I realized that he probably talked about this kind of stuff every day. It was no big deal to him.

"If there are so many aliens here, why do they stay a secret?"

"Almost every human has met an alien at one time or another," he informed me. "Most aliens don't try very hard to hide what they are. But most humans don't even notice. They're too busy, or they pretend that it didn't happen so that other people don't think they're crazy. Most humans are not ready to admit, even to themselves, that aliens exist."

"I can see why, if the aliens are all like Mathis," I said with a shiver.

My grandfather shook his head.

"No, most of them are like your friend Sylvie," he explained. "Very much like us, just trying to get by."

Sylvie.

A half hour after the Jupiterians left, while Elliot and I were watching the Amalgam Labs folks vacuum up every speck of dirt around the portable, we had found Sylvie sitting by herself. She had her knees pulled up to her chest and her hooded head buried in her arms.

"He didn't come," she said, rocking back and forth slightly.

"Who?" I asked. Even though I was pretty sure I knew.

"My dad," Sylvie confirmed, still rocking. "I thought he would. But he didn't even respond to my messages."

"Is he someone important?" I asked, remembering suddenly that

Mathis had mentioned Sylvie's father. If Mathis had known who he was, he must be someone prominent.

"He *is* a restaurateur. I didn't lie," Sylvie said, raising her head slightly to look at me. "But he's also the Chancellor in Charge of Martian-Human Affairs. It's his job to investigate and arrest people like Mathis."

"Oh," I said. "So that's why you were so interested in the whole thing…"

Sylvie shook her head.

"At first, I thought Mathis was after you. Hybrids are big business in the illegal pet trade. They just weren't *Mathis's* business. I didn't know that until the night we broke into her office."

"And when you knew she wasn't after me…" I encouraged her.

Sylvie shrugged.

"She was still a smuggler. I thought if I told my dad, he would come to Earth and arrest her. And I could see him. I haven't, you know. Seen him. Since my parents separated."

Sylvie's lower lip quivered, and my heart went out to my alien friend.

"I wrote and told him about Mathis, but he didn't respond. So then I thought, what if *I* captured her *for* him? Then he'd *really* have to come here. And maybe…"

Her voice faltered, and she drew in a ragged sigh.

"Maybe he'd be proud of you?" I suggested, finishing her thought.

Sylvie nodded and angrily swatted away a tear.

"It's stupid. He doesn't care. He just let my mom take me to Earth. Now he wants nothing to do with me. He didn't write me back. I don't think he ever will."

My grandfather, who had been walking up behind us, paused at Sylvie's words.

"You haven't heard from your father since you came to Earth?" he asked.

Sylvie shook her head.

My grandfather frowned.

"Curious," he said, and continued walking.

"It doesn't matter," Sylvie said, sniffing once and holding her head up high. "I don't need him."

"Yeah!" Elliot said, slapping her encouragingly on the back. "That's the spirit! Good riddance!"

Sylvie doubled over from the strength of Elliot's slap. When she sat up straight again, she had a watery smile on her face.

"Yeah," she repeated. "Good riddance."

I was pretty sure Sylvie would be OK. I, for one, was glad she had come to Earth. And even gladder that she was going to stay.

Back in my living room, my grandfather put down his salad and fixed me with a serious look.

"I'm sorry I didn't get here sooner," he said. "I have been in mandatory post-mission decontamination for the past two months. I came the moment I got your emails this morning."

"That's OK," I assured him. "Thanks for coming today, though. We wouldn't have known what to do with Mathis, once we sprayed her."

"We have Ms. Helen to thank for that," he told me. "I went to look for you at school, but it was Ms. Helen who led me to the portables. I gather she's been helping you all along?"

I nodded. "But I still don't understand why. I never got the feeling she liked me, or any of us, very much. She never talks." And I suspected that, no matter what Sylvie said, there had to be more to it than Ms. Helen just really, really liking Mrs. Juarez's flan.

My grandfather smiled.

"I'm sure Ms. Helen likes you fine. But I think she is also hoping that by helping you, word of her good deeds will get back to the Martian High Council. Ms. Helen is in politics, you know. She's from Pluto. And the Plutonians have a lot to prove these days. Ever since they lost their planetary status and all."

Pluto? Well, I guess that explained why the front office was always so cold...

My grandfather sat forward.

"Before I forget, I have something for you."

He reached into his shirt pocket and extracted a vial. He held it up to the light, so I could see that it was three-quarters full of blue liquid.

"Is that..." I trailed off.

"A cure, yes."

"But—" I squeaked. "Mom said you were five years away from human testing..."

"We are," my grandfather said. "At least when it comes to *formal* human testing. *Informal* human tests have been going on for years at Amalgam Labs. As you might have guessed, from the change in my appearance since the last time we met."

I couldn't take my eyes off the blue vial. A cure. A *real* cure. Exactly what I'd been looking for since the first day of school.

My grandfather tapped the vial, making the blue liquid slosh around.

"This is what I took, five years ago," he told me. "It is one hundred percent effective. But it is also irreversible. Once you take it—*if* you take it—you will never be able to turn your dinosaur genes on again. So you must be sure."

He took my hand and placed the vial in it.

"Think about it for a while," my grandfather suggested, as he sat back in his chair to finish his salad.

I took the rubber top off the vial and sniffed, curiously.

It had no scent. Not even to my ultrasensitive dino nose.

What would happen if I drank it? What if, when the dinosaur parts were gone, I went right back to being who I used to be? The Sawyer who never spoke up, never stood up for himself? Who hoped nobody would ever notice him? That Sawyer wouldn't have tried to save a portable full of kids from aliens.

And what else would be different? I thought about that day on the soccer field, when I had turned into the wind. I thought about the feel of the sun on my plates, the icy chill of the breeze. About the mouthwatering scent of freshly cut greens. And how the smell changed to a spicy nuttiness when they had molé sauce poured on them.

Would any of those things be the same, once I was just plain old Sawyer again?

I had come so far. The skin on the underside of my tail had toughened up, so it no longer hurt to drag my tail around. I hardly ever lost tennis balls off the ends of my spikes on accident anymore. And my mom had finished altering all of my clothes to fit over my dinosaur parts. I didn't quite have the roaring thing under control, but I was sure that I'd figure that out too. Eventually.

I jammed the rubber stopper back into the tube and looked up at my grandfather.

He was smiling. He put down his salad bowl and leaned forward. For a long moment, he just examined my face.

"You stood into the wind, didn't you?" he said finally.

I nodded.

My grandfather's smile changed from knowing to wistful. He put his hand very lightly on my topmost plate.

"I miss that. Sometimes, I wish…"

He trailed off, and I knew he was thinking about the day he had drunk whatever was in that tube. What had prompted him to make that choice?

I would have to remember to ask him sometime.

He cleared his throat and sat back against the couch cushions.

"You keep that," he said. "Just in case you change your mind one day."

I nodded and put the vial into my pocket.

Later, before I went to bed, I put the vial on the very top of my bookcase. Where I could still see it, but just barely.

It was nice to know I had it. Just in case. I'm only eleven, after all. A lot of things could happen in the future. Things that might make me decide I don't want to be part dinosaur anymore.

But right now, at this moment, I can't picture anything that would make me want to be someone else.

Like I always say, at least it isn't boring.

Never a dull moment.

Author's Note

Sawyer may be the only *actual* part-dinosaur in this story (aside from the stupid T. rex from New Jersey), but if you read very closely, you'll find dinosaurs (and the people who study them) all over this book.

The kids who make fun of Sawyer are all loosely based on carnivorous predators from the late Jurassic period that might have harassed a real *Stegosaurus*. Cici, with her prominent nose and dedication to the swim team, is based on *Ceratosaurus*, a theropod dinosaur with a large horned nose who likely spent a lot of time in the water. Parker, with his long face and birdlike build, is similar to *Pterodactylus* (commonly called a pterodactyl, and which, I feel compelled to point out, is actually a pterosaur—not a dinosaur—but still extremely cool). And Allan, with his large head, smallish arms, and penchant for eating meat, is based on *Allosaurus*, a dinosaur that looked a lot like a smallish version of *T. rex* and which paleontologists believe was *Stegosaurus*'s main predator. (Allan's last name, "Huxley," is a nod to Thomas Henry

Huxley, who laid early groundwork for the theory that birds may have evolved from dinosaurs.)

Sawyer's dog, Fantasia, shares her name with a famous *Stegosaurus* fossil that was found in the death grips of an *Allosaurus* fossil. The *Stegosaurus* fossil was named Fantastia, and the *Allosaurus* fossil was named Dracula—the two of them together have been nicknamed "the fighting pair" and provided much of the inspiration for Sawyer and Allan's relationship.

Ms. Felch, Sawyer's homeroom teacher, is named for Marshall P. Felch who found the first *Stegosaurus* fossil in 1876. Mr. Broome, the computer teacher, is a reference to Broome, Australia, where a number of dinosaur footprints (which were considered sacred to the aboriginal population there) were stolen in 1996. Some of the prints have since been recovered, but the stegosaur ones are still at large. Coach Carpenter is named for Kenneth Carpenter, a.k.a. the "Indiana Jones of Bones," who, among other things, discovered the most complete *Stegosaurus* fossil ever found.

Dr. Dana from the Amalgam Labs video is named for the Dana Quarry in Wyoming, the site in the Morrison Formation where Fantasia and Dracula were found. The other two scientists in the video are named for Othniel Charles Marsh and Edward Drinker Cope, two paleontologists whose famous (and often hilarious) rivalry in the late nineteenth century was nicknamed "The Bone Wars." Marsh is credited with the discovery of the "type fossil" for *Stegosaurus*, and he also came up with the name "*Stegosaurus*" (as well as "*Allosaurus*," "*Triceratops*," and others).

Dr. Gilmore, Sawyer's vet, is named for Dr. Charles W.

Gilmore, a famous paleontologist who named one of the subspecies of *Stegosaurus* and who was a prominent figure during the Bone Wars. Sawyer's pediatrician, Dr. Bakker, was named for Dr. Robert Bakker who, along with his teacher, Dr. Ostrom, popularized the theory that birds are descended from dinosaurs and dinosaurs may have been warm-blooded.

Morrison, Colorado (the site of the fictional "Camp Remorse") is actually a town named after the famous Morrison Formation, where fossils have been discovered since 1877.

Gary Simmons, the "second tallest kid" in Sawyer's class, is an homage to my favorite Far Side cartoon (by Gary Larson) where cave-scientists name the *Stegosaurus*'s tail the "thagomizer" in honor of "the late Thag Simmons." (I wanted to name the kid "Thag," but honestly, when was the last time you met someone named "Thag"?)

There are a few other references in this book. To some things that are more "extra" than "terrestrial," which hint at Sylvie's origins as well as to where we are headed in the next Dinosaur Boy book. But I'll leave it to you to find those (*cough,* Dr. Cook's lecture on the science fair, *cough*) and save my explanations for *Dinosaur Boy Saves Mars...*

Much love (and dinosaur-sized hugs),

CPO

Acknowledgments

I am forever indebted to the following individuals for making this book a reality:

My amazing husband, Mark Oakes, for being my ultimate support and my partner in all things. And our kiddos, Sophia and Alex, for so generously sharing Mommy with her imaginary friends.

My agent, Sarah LaPolla, who not only championed this book but also inspired it, in a one-line email late one Friday night. (That's right, she's that awesome.)

My editor, Aubrey Poole, and everybody at Sourcebooks for giving this book such a loving home. I can't imagine a better place for *Dinosaur Boy* to have landed. Thanks especially to Becca Sage, the production editor, and her team for putting up with my annoying dinosaur nomenclature issues. Thanks to editorial assistant Kate Prosswimmer for all her support; Melanie Jackson, for her amazing work on the internal design of this book; Will Riley, for his work on the cover; and to Kathryn Lynch for all of her hard work.

Kristen Lipscomb Sund, my friend and a genetic counselor at Cincinnati Children's Hospital Medical Center, for talking me through some of the finer points of genetics. She deserves all of the credit for any real science that may have snuck into this book (and none of the blame for the stuff that I made up!).

The awesome-beyond-description writing community of Austin, Texas, for taking me under their collective wing and making an author of me. Especially Cynthia Leitich Smith for her guidance, her fabulousness, and her willingness to eat weird cheese with me. And Greg Leitich Smith for always talking "dinosaur" with me at parties.

All of my ladies from the "Lodge of Death" who saw this story grow from a quirky idea to an actual, real, live book. Especially Nikki Loftin (the tennis balls were her idea!), Madeline Smoot (for helping me through some tricky, early plotting), and Mari Mancusi (for being such a stellar writing buddy).

And finally, thank *you*, for picking up this book. I hope you enjoyed reading it at least half as much as I enjoyed writing it!

About the Author

Cory Putman Oakes was born in Basel, Switzerland, but grew up outside of San Francisco, California. She earned her BA (in psychology) from the University of California at Los Angeles, and her JD from Cornell Law School, and then naturally decided to pursue a profession that utilized neither of these. Her first book, *The Veil*, a young adult fantasy, was published in 2011, and she is proud to be making her middle grade debut with *Dinosaur Boy*.

Cory lives in Austin, Texas, with her husband, kids, and pets. She knew nothing about dinosaurs before she started writing this book, but now she can tell a sauropod from a theropod. She also makes a mean molé sauce. You can often find Cory on Twitter (@CoryPutmanOakes) and Facebook, and you can learn more about her (and her books) on her website: www.corypoakes.com.

Don't miss Dinosaur Boy's next adventure:

DINOSAUR BOY SAVES MARS

Sawyer and his two best friends are on a rescue mission to Mars when they encounter bullying on a galactic scale: Mars is trying to kick Pluto out of the solar system.

While searching for Sylvie's missing father, Sawyer, Elliot, and Sylvie find themselves part of an intergalactic mess. Apparently, solar system squabbles are solved by soccer games! The upcoming Mars vs. Pluto soccer match will decide the fate of both planets—but the trio of Earthlings discover that there's a secret plot to sabotage the game, one that puts the whole galaxy in danger. It's up to Sawyer to save the day...as only a part-stegosaurus (with a taste for Tex-Mex) can.